In Over Your Head

Attack on Times Square Y2k

Eugene L. Welischar

authorHOUSE®

AuthorHouse™
1663 Liberty Drive
Bloomington, IN 47403
www.authorhouse.com
Phone: 1 (800) 839-8640

Photographer of the cover image: Timothy R. Wildey

Published by AuthorHouse 02/16/2015

ISBN: 978-1-4969-6758-9 (sc)
ISBN: 978-1-4969-6759-6 (hc)
ISBN: 978-1-4969-6757-2 (e)

Library of Congress Control Number: 2015901590

Print information available on the last page.

CONTENTS

ACKNOWLEDGMENTS

- To Ellen, my lifetime partner, without whom I could not have completed my two books.

- To Ann, my daughter, who designed my book covers; her research and finishing touches were invaluable.

- To my dynamic trio--Dr. Peg Stengel, Judy Sibley and Debbie Park--for their enthusiastic encouragement and insightful critique.

- To Professor Dan Brady and his wife, Sue, for their help and interest in my projects.

- To Ray Powers, retired NYPD Inspector, who gave me valuable information on 1999 personnel and procedures.

- To Richie Fuerch, retired FDNY Deputy Chief, who also gave me the 1999 make-up of personnel and procedures.

- To Janet Kimmerly, a knowledgeable FDNY civilian employee and editor of *WNYF* (*With New York Firefighters*), who assisted me with editing.

- To Frank Montagna, retired FDNY Battalion Chief, who helped so much with his professional input and suggestions.

- To James Sheehan, published author of five mystery novels, for his advice, input and constructive critique of my work.

IN MEMORY OF SHAWN GRIFFITH

This book is in memory of Shawn Griffith, whose editing and research skills were instrumental in developing this book. Unfortunately, demons, bad luck and being an ex-felon closed many doors to him. A parole violation landed him in jail again and he lost all hope of achieving his potential to the point of committing suicide. Our paths crossed in Florida and our relationship became one of father and son.

Shawn was a young man who made a terrible mistake; he robbed an ATM and possessed a gun when caught. For those crimes, he paid a steep price, more than 20 years in prison.

He paid his debt to society, but he did more than that. Experiencing, enduring and surviving prison life, he sought to improve conditions for those who might follow.

He self-published a book, *Facing the U.S. Prison Problem, 2.3 Million Strong, an Ex-Con's View of the Mistakes and Solutions*, which addresses recidivism rates and problems within the prison system. After earning college credits from Ohio University, Shawn became an acknowledged prison teacher, helping more than 300 inmates obtain their GED.

Despite his hope and desire to complete his journey, he ran into many roadblocks. As an ex-felon, potential employers would not hire him. Despair and depression set in. He was stopped by the police and they found drugs in his car. This was in violation of his parole. He was sentenced to three more years.

In the end, at 43 years old, prison life sapped Shawn's dreams and ultimately took his way-too-short life. He committed suicide on May 3, 2014, while in prison. I hope he receives the peace within that he sought. I will feel his loss for the rest of my life.

PREFACE

Women wanted equal opportunity in employment. They were expected to be mothers and homemakers in the '50s and '60s, but many also had to become providers as single mothers and heads of households. The economy was bad and good paying jobs were few. They wanted entry into the New York City Fire Department and the job security it provided. Heretofore, they were not allowed entry, but that changed in the '80s.

The test used for admittance to the New York City Fire Department consisted of two parts, one written and the other physical. All candidates handled the first part well, but the second part posed problems. The litigation ordering the City to open the Fire Department ranks to females was anticipated, so the City jumped the gun to implement the process before it became law. However, the City developed a physical that was so tough, only a few females passed, and the percentage of men who passed was half of what it had been previously.

As a result, female candidates petitioned the courts that the test was unfair and the City had deliberately made it tough so that few women could pass. The petition went to a judge who, unfortunately, had no comprehension of the issues and lowered the passing mark on the physical test for women only. This ruling resulted in monumental problems. It catapulted women on the already promulgated list over men who had passed and were on the list for new hires. The war between the sexes had begun.

When women were appointed to openings in the Fire Department, they were met with nasty reactions from the Firemen, particularly newer ones, whose brothers and friends on the list were now passed over. Some women were not included in meals and social functions in the firehouse. Their equipment went missing; a few even had dog feces placed in their boots.

It was a sad and disturbing situation and the City came down hard and swiftly on the Firemen. If they did not desist, they would be fired.

The women who passed the severely lowered physical tests could not do the job and, gradually, they were siphoned off into desk jobs, with silent approval from the City to prevent any additional court cases.

Gradually, through the years, the system corrected itself, but the general opinion among many Firemen remained that most women could not perform the extreme physical aspects of the job due to their lack of upper body strength. Eventually, the tests were adjusted and made fair for both men and women in judging their physical strength.

# # #

CHAPTER 1

Spring, 1999. Mary Walsh was awake at 4:30 a.m., too excited to sleep.

She lay in bed and thought of her first 9-to-6 day tour as a detailed Lieutenant at Ladder 115 in Long Island City. She had been a covering Officer for nine long months since her promotion to Lieutenant. Now, she possibly had landed a permanent assignment at Ladder 115 because the regularly assigned Lieutenant had been injured and placed on long-term medical leave.

Mary felt she might have finally gotten her lucky break at a permanent assignment.

She took a mental inventory of her firefighting equipment: helmet, boots, a Nomex fireproof turnout coat and flashlight; also, her changes of clothing and toiletries. Did she forget anything?

Mary decided to get out of bed because her thoughts were racing, and the butterflies in her stomach were on a rampage, though she had placed all she needed in the trunk of her car the night before to ward off these first-day jitters.

Now fully dressed, she went back out to her car in the driveway. The sound of the early birds beginning to chirp gave her a reassuring sense of not being alone. She checked her equipment and returned to her apartment satisfied she had not forgotten anything.

Nine-year-old Toni-Ann, Mary's daughter, shared the two-bedroom apartment with her in Levittown, Long Island, where she had grown up. Levittown, not too far from New York City, was originally one of those first housing developments built by the Levitt Brothers in the late 1940s for returning GIs.

The small, uniform, box-like homes in the suburbs were advertised as the "American Dream" and sold for less than $5,000. Trees lined the curving streets, two to each front yard.

These days, most of the houses had been expanded and modernized over the decades to accommodate middle class families and baby boomers.

She put coffee on and prepared her favorite breakfast -- a toasted English muffin with cream cheese and marmalade. This helped calm the butterflies in her stomach.

Mary already had arranged babysitting for her two upcoming day tours and dropped Toni-Ann off the previous night with her best friend, Sheila.

Sheila, a nurse who worked rotating shifts, also had a daughter Alexandra, the same age as Toni-Ann. The girls were in fourth grade and went to Wisdom Lane Elementary School together.

Sheila and Mary worked out their schedules so they could babysit for each other. If that didn't work out, the girls' grandmothers were eager to fill in and watch their granddaughters when both moms were working.

She took her coffee to the picnic table on the small patio just outside her side door. Daylight was just arriving and she reflected on the nine years since Toni was born.

Mary's daughter was born out of wedlock when she was 19. Toni's father was the same age. Early on, it became evident Toni's dad could not cope with the heavy responsibility of fatherhood. He was out of the picture and Mary was on her own.

One thing Mary knew absolutely was that she loved her little girl and would raise Toni the best she possibly could on her own. She expected it to be tough, but she was determined to do it right. Thankfully, she lived at home with her mother, Pat, which helped things out immensely.

Still pregnant, Mary signed up for a two year Licensed Practical Nurse program offered at the Nassau BOCES technical school nearby. While attending school, Mary ran into her childhood friend, Sheila, in one of her nursing classes. Sheila had just recently given birth to her own daughter, Alexandra, also out of wedlock, and was living at home with her mother.

After Toni-Ann was born and after Mary graduated and passed her LPN test, she began working at a medical center in Hicksville. Sheila, too, became an LPN and started a job at Nassau County Medical Center.

With their renewed friendship and common bonds, Mary and Sheila shared their responsibilities as young, single moms working as nurses. Toni-Ann and Alex developed their own "best friends" relationship.

Within two years, Mary and Sheila decided to strike out on their own. They found apartments near each other and became a solid team, raising the girls and pursuing their careers. Sheila went back to school, became an RN, and was a Nurse Manager at the hospital where she worked. Mary decided to follow her father's footsteps and courageously entered into the New York City Fire Department under her dad's tutelage.

Gene Walsh, a retired Captain in the FDNY, was integral in guiding Mary as she studied hard, did well on the written test and physical, and became one of the small handful of female Firefighters in the City. In six years, securing incremental raises, Mary had become a first-grade Firefighter, which made her eligible to take the Lieutenants test.

During this time, Mary once again studied hard for the exam with her father's help. They would get together several times a month and go over the scheduled subjects. Mary enrolled in Delehanty's school of study for promotional civil service exams. When the Lieutenants test became available, she was ready. Mary knocked it dead and was on the top of the list.

Team Mary and Sheila, with their two Probies, Toni-Ann and Alexandra, had done exceptionally well for themselves.

CHAPTER 2

Anticipating the 30 mile drive to Long Island City, Queens, on a Friday when traffic usually was heavy, Mary left about two hours before her tour was scheduled to begin. As she drove, she thought about her path to becoming first a Firefighter, and now a Lieutenant.

She had experienced the entry of women into the Fire Department in its insipient stages and she was well aware of all the logistical problems having to do with testing politics and the rigorous physicality of the job. As far as she was concerned, though, she was well-qualified mentally and physically, and destined to become a Fireman.

Mary and her dad were always extremely close. As a little girl growing up, she had spent many days and sometimes sleepover nights in the firehouse. A tomboy, Mary had fit in well with all the Firemen. Softball games, picnics and Christmas parties were just a few of the many functions she participated in.

Mary and her favorite Fireman, John Thomasion, had a magic show together and performed for many firehouse Christmas parties. The classic disappearing rabbit was one of their favorite acts and the children loved it.

As a young teen, Mary went to outdoor training drills with her dad's tower-ladder company and learned how to operate its' bucket high above the street. The control handle was very sensitive, much like the joysticks on video games Mary had played so often in neighborhood stores back then.

Fireman Bill Hardy, who took Mary up in the bucket, said she was a natural. It was even suggested that some of the younger Firemen, who were intimidated by the tower ladder controls, practice their fine motor skills by playing video games, too.

On the rides back and forth to the firehouse and her dad's apartment, Mary would question everything about the happenings of that day. And now, her thoughts fast-forwarded to the present, she was a Lieutenant!

She wrenched herself from the fond memories of her dad and the Fire Department and focused on the present. She wanted to be fully alert on the first day of her new assignment.

Approaching the historic firehouse now, which housed her new Ladder Company, Engine Company and the Battalion Chief and his Aide, Mary noted the character and makeup of the Italian neighborhood with its' old City flavor. Her dad had told her it was a very safe community, the "old guard" families made sure of that.

Arriving early as anticipated, Mary noticed her hands fumble as she opened the door and entered.

Yes, she had to admit, she was a little nervous.

The housewatchman jumped to his feet to greet Mary. He had known she was coming. All the Firefighters speculated on what the new female Lieutenant would be like. Mary noted his enthusiastic demeanor and how young he looked with his curly red hair and fresh scrubbed face.

"Fireman Albin is my name. Welcome to Ladder 115," he greeted her friendly, extending his hand.

Chris Albin was also a second generation Firefighter.

"Thanks, I'm Lieutenant Mary Walsh," she returned the handshake.

"The Captain said he'd be down in a moment. Want a cup of coffee"?

"Yes, I would like one. Thank you."

Fireman Albin escorted Mary toward the kitchen and as she walked behind him through the apparatus floor, she overheard two Firemen working on the opposite side of the fire truck. As she passed, she overheard a remark from one them.

"After all my 20 years on the job, we never had a female assigned here. What's this job comin' to is what I want to know"!

As Mary entered the kitchen, she pretended not to hear the comment. She knew that a lot of Firemen were bitter about females on the job. As far as she was concerned, though, the debate was over and the outcome remained the same--female firefighters were here to stay, regardless of the views of some of the disgruntled veterans. Plus, Mary always handled the bias in the past by focusing on being an exemplary Firefighter and earning the men's respect. And she was just as determined to stick to that philosophy now as an Officer.

Mary was sitting down with her mug of coffee when the Captain entered, his hand outstretched.

"Welcome aboard, Mary! I'm Captain Piegere. I worked as a Fireman with your father when he was a Lieutenant at Engine 218 in Brooklyn. You look just like him."

He smiled at Mary, pulled up a chair and sat down.

"The last time I talked to Gene was when he had that shootout with an arsonist ages ago. I got in touch with him back then and he filled me in on some of the particulars of the incident," he reflected and paused. "But, except for a few chance meetings at wakes and promotional parties, I lost track of him. I knew from Department Orders he retired about 10 years ago.

"Back in the day, we were a really busy, close-knit unit in 218. I often wondered how life was treating Gene. How's he doing and how's your mother, Pat? We had many good times together"!

"My mom and dad divorced in the late '70s when I was 10 years old. It didn't work out, but, they've remained friends throughout the years," Mary responded politely.

"I know he owned a bar and restaurant in Long Beach," said Captain Piegere. "My wife and I have eaten there. Great place. The Inn! I remember it was in the West End of town, on Tennessee Avenue."

"Yes, he still lives there, down the block from the bar. I see Dad pretty often and he'll be very glad to know I met you."

Sensing her anxious excitement at walking into a new firehouse, just as he had when he was a new Lieutenant, he wanted to make Mary feel at ease in her new role. After all, the firehouse would be her second home.

The Captain grabbed a cup of coffee for himself and made informal introductions to some of the men assembled for their morning coffee. There was the usual easy flowing firehouse banter.

Captain Piegere then took Mary upstairs to the company office and took time to familiarize her with some routines and the riding list of the men working her tour.

"Mary, whenever you're ready to take over, let me know. I wouldn't mind leaving early. I'm driving up to the College at New Paltz today to pick up my son for the weekend."

Mary hid her excitement and tried to ignore the butterflies in her stomach which began to flutter once again.

"I'm as ready as I'll ever be, Cap. Thanks for your help," she said, briefly wondering if she appeared like a foolish schoolgirl on the first day of school.

"Have a good first day, Lou, and I'll see you on the next day tour. Your relief tonight will be Lieutenant Tom Murphy and he'll fill you in on some more of our standard routines. Good luck"! he called after her and left the office.

She appreciated first impressions and quickly summed up the Captain -- broad-shouldered, gray hair, penetrating blue eyes, soft-spoken but direct, easy-going but confident. A man she would be happy to report to.

She went down to the apparatus floor a little before 9:00 a.m. to put her gear in the cab of the ladder truck. After taking out the Captain's equipment and returning it to his assigned space, she met with the crew and introduced herself. She gave the Firemen their assignments from the riding list that the Captain prepared for her. She then walked around the aerial ladder to familiarize herself with it and see where the tiller man would sit on the top of the rear ladder.

The tiller man would steer in unison with the chauffeur driving the truck. For the most part, this type of apparatus had been phased out of the Fire Department, but a few still were needed where old streets and corners were narrow and small. Old locations, such as downtown New York and various other sections of the City, needed these units where the back end of the ladder could be flexible enough to make the short turns.

The voice alarm came to life with a message. Mary felt her heart jump as her adrenaline kicked into action.

"Box 7248, Queens Boulevard and 46th Street, a reported fire in a furniture store, a taxpayer building. All units acknowledge"!

"Ladder 115, Engine 258, Battalion 45, *10-4*," the housewatchman responded.

CHAPTER 3

Immediately, all her men took their riding positions on the truck and followed Engine 258 out of quarters with the 45th Battalion Chief's car following. A reported taxpayer fire triggered a mental picture for Mary. Most of the one-story buildings were built in the 1930s during the Depression and made up of cheap construction with rows of connected stores which typically ran the length of a block.

Their low building cost enabled owners and renters to pay their taxes and also make a living. These units became known as "taxpayers" and as their success and popularity grew, many were built into the '40s and '50s.

The problem was that they had a three-foot cockloft below the roof and above the store ceilings. This common space ran the whole length of the building creating the potential for one huge conflagration of flames. In other words, the block-long structures went up like tinderboxes if not swiftly extinguished.

All members knew the routine attack plan for taxpayer fires. Carrying it out was another story. Specifically, the problems -- visual late discovery of the fire in the stores during the night, the common cockloft and the direction of the wind -- could cause the fire to take off with amazing speed.

Pulling ceilings, opening roofs in adjoining stores, keeping hose-lines available and getting ahead of the fast-traveling fire, was a precise and very physically demanding operation. If the Firemen could stop the fire in the original store, pull adjoining ceilings and open those roofs, they could stop the spread. If not, the fire would develop into a spectacular blaze.

Approaching Queens Boulevard, the fire crew saw large plumes of smoke in the sky. Mary was charged up but remembered something her dad often told her:

> *"When going to a fire, realize that the excitement will cause an adrenaline rush, speeding up your thoughts and actions. Slow everything down to keep your metabolism normal. This will help in your decision-making, plus with normal breathing, your air mask will last much longer."*

Mary reported to the Chief of Battalion 45 for orders.

"Lou, take exposure #2, the shop to the left of the furniture store on fire. The wind seems to be blowing in that direction, so pull the ceilings and open the roof to try and cut it off," he responded.

Mary and her forcible entry team entered exposure #2. They were followed by Engine 258, carrying a charged hose-line. Her roof and outside vent man, assisted by the chauffeur, placed a portable ladder to the one-story roof. They climbed to the roof with their gas-powered saw, an axe and a hook.

Knowing the fire was in the rear, they opened a 10 by 10 foot hole over where they expected the fire to travel, to vent the smoke and heat to the outside. Inside the store, as Mary and her men were groping through smoke and heat to get to the rear, they heard the sounds of the saw opening the roof.

When the roof was opened up, conditions immediately got better as visibility improved and heat dissipated. Both companies quickly advanced to the rear and feverishly pulled the ceilings down to expose the intense cockloft fire. The Firemen of Engine 258 quickly opened their hose-line with a strong, penetrating stream and extinguished all visible fire.

Meanwhile, Mary swiftly directed her team as they pulled ceilings in other areas of the store. They exposed more fire and in unison with the engine company, they extinguished the advancing flames.

Mary began to feel relief wash over her as her company continued to open ceilings and make safety checks. Soon after, all visible fire was extinguished in the cockloft.

"I think we have it under control. Great job, men"! The Chief announced after he entered the store and saw the results.

"Keep looking for any pockets of fire."

He was pleased with their performance and later, the Chief came back again to check.

"Looks good."

He turned to his aide in tow.

"Give a 'fire under control' report to the Chief in Charge."

He turned back to the two companies -- Ladder 115 and Engine 258 -- and gave a thumbs-up.

"Go out and take a break. Other relieving companies are just arriving."

The Firemen walked out, sweaty and exhausted, and headed over to Engine 258's pumper where the chauffeur had connected a water spigot to one of its outlets. They all began removing their heavy, water-logged turnout coats and drank plenty of water to replace the fluids the extreme heat had extracted from their bodies. Some put their heads and shoulders under the cold fountain of water. At that point, Mary couldn't have cared less about what her hair looked like.

"Take up and take an hour's rest back at quarters. Good job"! The Chief advised soon after.

He was an authoritative but amiable man, giving the Firemen well-deserved *"atta boys"* to validate the crew's high spirits after their dangerous and a well-executed performance.

CHAPTER 4

The crew rode back to quarters recapping their efforts with animated gestures.

Fireman Albin was getting hungry.

"What's for lunch"? he chirped from his seat in back of the chauffeur and the senior man, Tom Dunn.

"How about we stop at Harry's for heroes? Albin, count how many we need for the engine crew, the Chief and us."

"Heroes it is! We'll get three different types for everyone. Oh boy, time for lunch"! the perpetually hungry Albin clapped, grinning like a Cheshire cat.

Pulling up to Harry's, Albin and three other men jumped off the rig.

As they waited for lunch, Tom Dunn filled Mary in on the history of Harry's Italian Grocery.

"Harry Galleo is a legend. He retired from Ladder 116 in the late '70's and decided to buy this deli when the previous owner retired. He was a gourmet cook in the firehouse for over 30 years. He made all the food for the retirement and promotion parties, too.

"This deli was a natural for him. I'd say he's had it about 15 years now. He must be about eighty years old and still going strong. It's a labor of love," Dunn smiled.

"Harry caters lots of parties and events here, too. There's an outdoor bocce court in the rear and he has tables and chairs for eating and drinking. His patrons play bocce or play cards, dominoes… He makes his own homemade vino, too. Harry's a genuine throw-back to the old days"!

At that point, Harry came out from the store and approached Tom.

"They told me about the fire, Tom. Thank God nobody got hurt! I'll have my man deliver sandwiches to the firehouse in about a half hour. That's okay"? Harry asked.

Harry was born in Italy, moved to New York as a young boy, and still had an accent.

"Sure thing, Harry. Thanks." replied Dunn.

"You won't believe this coincidence," Mary commented afterward.

"My father, Gene, was a Fireman in Ladder 116 before I was born and I remember him telling me stories about 116 and Harry. Pretty amazing to meet him now!"

When they all returned to their quarters, Mary was glad a relocated company was there to answer additional calls for their area. The relocated company already had lunch and this uninterrupted time to shower and collect her thoughts was a blessing.

After dressing, Mary sat down at the office desk and began completing the required reports on the taxpayer fire. Soon after, the house watchman gave a shout over the intercom.

"Chow's on"!

The hero sandwiches had been delivered and were unwrapped and cut in thirds because they were so big. This gave the men an enticing selection to enjoy.

Mary was delighted. The fire had been purposeful in the scheme of things and this repast, with everyone feeling good about their accomplishment, was a pivotal moment for her. Mary hoped the initial ice had been broken with her new company, and that she was on her way to being accepted as their Lieutenant.

When the men finished their lunch, Mary addressed the relocated company.

"We're all set to go here. Take up when you're ready."

Later that day, two false alarms and an electrical emergency completed Mary's first day tour. At 5:00 p.m., she went down to the kitchen to meet some of the incoming tour and to share the riding list with Lieutenant Murphy. The incoming night tour of approximately 15 men, added to her day tour, which meant about 25 men coming together for tour change.

Mary's firehouse background definitely helped prevent her from feeling overly intimidated by this large group of Firemen. Though she still felt nervous, she knew what to expect.

While pouring herself a cup of coffee, she was approached by Lieutenant Murphy,

"Hi, I'm your relief, Tom Murphy. How was your first day? I heard about the fire."

"The men did a great job," Mary said standing up to greet him.

He was Black Irish with tanned skin, deep brown eyes and wavy brown hair. With a tall and lean, athletic build, she found it hard to maintain focus on his eyes without noticing his natural good looks and physique.

She sat down with Tom and the other Firemen. Mary always felt this was the most enjoyable part of the tour, filled with conversation and lighthearted dialogue. Afterward, Tom got up, nodded to Mary and they both headed for their office.

He showed her some more procedures and the locations of pertinent materials she would need. Conversation seemed to move easily between them.

"Give me a few minutes to change into my work clothes and I'll be ready to relieve you," he said.

"Okay," Mary answered and went to her own dressing area.

In the few minutes alone, she wondered if he was single, but quickly put the thought out of her mind. When he was ready, Tom returned to the office.

"All set, Mary. See you tomorrow morning"!

"Okay, Tom, have a good night."

Her ride home was therapeutic as she recounted the events of her first day. She concluded it had gone well and was eager to fill her dad in. She'd tell him all about the fire and meeting Harry Galleo. She'd also mention the Fireman who unwittingly dissed her. She wasn't really upset with the guy, a senior man. She'd just ignore any negative remarks on the topic of gender discrimination.

Mary also learned something about men as a woman who grew up in firehouses. The less she made an issue of the men's bias and the more she focused on high standards and job performance, the more likely she would earn their respect.

Mary had faith in the general goodness of most Firemen and believed that this senior man eventually would come around. Time would tell, she thought to herself, as she pulled into her driveway, ready for a restful evening with Toni-Ann.

CHAPTER 5

Mary drove home Saturday evening after finishing her first two day tours at Ladder 115. The second day tour of her new assignment turned out to be quiet with only some expected new-job stress. Overall, Mary was very pleased with how she handled the new job.

She was off 48 hours until a 6-to-9 night tour Tuesday night and Wednesday morning. Now for a relaxing Saturday night with Toni-Ann, her precocious, animated daughter, who was so delightful to be around! She anticipated this precious time with her and looked forward to their traditional Sunday line-up tomorrow. After 10:00 folk mass at St. Bernard's, they would go to the Colony Diner for a late breakfast. Toni-Ann always ordered silver dollar pancakes.

Afterward, they would head out to Wantagh Park, as Mary had done so many times as a little girl with her dad, spending hours on the monkey bars and swings. Mary would end her playtime in the park's multi-colored concrete maze where she always had fun trying to find her way out.

One day, Mary's dad had gone into the maze and started to playfully chase her. Excitedly running away from him at full speed, Mary ran face first into a yellow brick wall. She bounced backward landing on her bottom, an emerging bump on her forehead. Though she was okay after a good cry and consoling hugs, Mary's dad felt terrible so when they left the park for ice cream treats at a nearby Carvel, he told her she could have anything she wanted. Both he and Mary felt much better after a decadent banana split.

Years later, the ice cream was just as yummy. Mary felt the same joy, only now it was in seeing her own daughter delight in what Mary had done so for many years past.

That Sunday evening, Sheila brought Alex to stay overnight before she went off to work her nightshift at the hospital. Mary was grateful for the system Sheila and she had worked out, which even enabled the single mothers to enjoy a night out for themselves once in a while.

Monday morning after taking the girls to school, Mary was savoring a second cup of coffee when the phone rang. It was her friend, Carol. She and Carol used to love getting dressed up and going to the various clubs to dance with their friends.

At one of the clubs, Carol met Abdul Hassam, Abby for short, and her life had changed. They fell in love and a year later, became engaged and decided to get an apartment together in Middle Village, Queens. Within the same neighborhood, Abby and his brother, Abraham, worked at a vehicle repair shop owned by the eldest brother, Mohammed.

Abby assimilated nicely into the New York atmosphere and American culture. He loved the Jets and other sports; he was even starting to play golf. Abby was crazy about Carol or at least he seemed so.

The only fly in the ointment was Abby's loyalty to his culturally rigid Muslim family. At first, he believed he could break the mold and marry a Christian girl. Although Islamic law banned inter-faith marriages in many cases, despite his apprehensions, Abby asked Carol to live with him.

Carol was crying and between sobs, managed to explain to Mary what had happened.

"Yesterday Abby's mother and father arrived here from Lebanon on a mission to destroy us," her words were breaking up.

"They wanted me to leave our apartment immediately! They insisted that Abby was not allowed to live with or marry a Christian girl. They said it was forbidden and that I was an infidel. I've never done anything but love their son"!

"Then when they saw the Jewish Mezuzah on the door frame that the last tenant left which I forgot to take down, they went ballistic! They wouldn't even let me explain to them that it wasn't mine. They kept shouting something about a *fat wash* or a *fatwa* or something. I don't even know..," she stammered.

"I just ran. They were acting like hysterical fanatics and I got scared.

"And Abby was no help, either! He just sat there cowering as they yelled at us. Mary, I don't think I can go back there again"! Carol blurted, sounding heartbroken.

"Where are you now"? asked Mary.

"I'm at my mother's house in Long Beach," Carol sniffled.

"But what about all of your stuff in the apartment? Don't you want to get it"?

"Yes, almost everything in the apartment is mine anyway; even the lease is in my name. I didn't know what to do so I called my sister, Barbara. As usual, she came up with a good plan. We're rounding up some girls and renting a van. We're all going over there tonight to get my stuff."

"Wow, I'm so sorry, Carol," Mary said empathetic.

"Sounds like a reasonable plan to me, Carol. If Abby didn't defend you and stand up to his radical family, it seems you deserve better. Count me in! I'm off, so I'll meet all of you at the apartment to help, too. What time will you be getting there"?

"Me, Barbara and my Mom should be there around seven with the van. So you, Gina, Christine and Meredith will have your cars which we'll use for stuff that won't fit in the van."

"Good, Sheila gets to my house around 5:30 this evening to pick up Alex. I'll have her take Toni-Ann home with her. So I'll see you at seven, then. Hang in there."

Mary hung up. She was disgusted by what she had just heard. Carol told her a while back that Abby and his brother, Abraham, were here on expired student visas and their older brother, Mohammed, who was married, had a green card. Mohammed had three children here with his American-born Muslim wife and rumor had it that he was married to another Muslim girl in Lebanon and had a family there.

Mohammed knew how to abuse the American system. Working mostly off the books at his garage made him eligible for medical assistance, food stamps and other government assistance. Despite the benefits of living in this country, Mohammed loathed the American system and basically thought that all Americans were stupid. He felt no allegiance to the U.S. whatsoever.

His American wife was fearful of Mohammed's physical abuse and once warned Carol she should be wary of what she was getting into; as for her, it was too late to extricate herself from her marriage to Mohammed. However, Carol had chosen to ignore the warning and other culture-related red flags because she was in love.

At 7:00 p.m., Mary pulled up to Carol and Abby's apartment where she was met by Gina, Christine and Meredith. They were all close friends for many years and were all boiling mad at Abby in their support for Carol. Just behind them, the van pulled up with Barbara driving, and Carol and Ellen, their mother, in the front seat.

In the apartment, Abby silently took his punishment from the girls who had plenty to say to him. Thankfully, his parents weren't at the apartment, they were with their grandchildren at Mohammed's house.

Abby admitted he could do nothing to reconcile the situation. He'd tried to break away from his culture but he was too submissive in nature, his family too overpowering in ideology.

Most of Carol's possessions were moved from the apartment in Queens to her mother's home in Long Beach. She decided to leave the furniture she bought with Abby in Middle Village.

After several hours of packing up, their work was done and on the way back to Ellen's house, the girls picked up pizza and a couple of six-packs of beer. Carol seemed a lot calmer with the move behind her and loving friends and family at her side.

However, when everybody left, Ellen held her as she cried. Words could not relieve a broken heart, but a mother's arms were comforting. Carol knew getting over Abby would not be easy.

CHAPTER 6

On Thursday, Mary left earlier for her night tour because she decided to stop at Abby's auto repair shop to speak with him. She wanted to get there before the garage closed for the day.

On the way, she recollected previous experiences with Abby and his brothers.

One morning, Mary had received a phone call from him.

"I have two tickets for today's Mets game against the Pirates and I can't make it. Would you and your father like to go? I know it's last-minute."

"Wow. I'm free today and I'll double check with my Dad, but I'm pretty sure he's also available. That would be great, Abby"! Mary responded with enthusiasm.

Mary called him right back with an okay from her dad and Abby gave her directions to the garage. She and her dad picked up the tickets and off they went to the game.

Mary's dad once helped Abby and his brothers reconcile several Fire Department summonses their shop had received. Mohammed never complied; instead, he threw the summonses in a drawer, ignoring them. Not long after, additional summonses arrived with penalties. Mohammed ignored them, too, and as a result, the shop had been hit with steep fines.

Mary had asked her father if he could help them. Gene was fond of Abby so he called his "hook" downtown to see if anything could be done. He told his friend that the Assam brothers were young, decent guys who just had no clue. His contact said that if they paid the original summonses immediately, something could possibly be done with the penalties. In the end, the summonses were paid and most of the late penalties were dropped.

Today, Mary's visit was filled with ambivalence, mostly disappointment and apprehension. Although Carol was ignorant to what a *fatwa* meant, Mary was aware of such hostile terms as *jihad* and *fatwa*.

When Mary arrived, she found the shop closed. A sign on the door read, "Moving to a New Location," and a contact number was listed beneath it. She jotted down the number which seemed familiar to her. Mary thought it could be the home number Abby had when he was staying with his brother, Abraham. She decided she would call the number in the morning after work.

Mary resumed her drive to work taking her time.

Approaching the firehouse, she liked to study the old firehouse. Each day, she noted another interesting characteristic of the building. The front was stepped Dutch gable, a Bradford Gilbert had designed it in 1903. He was known for designing and building railroad depots. Mary had just read about the building's history in an old newspaper clipping she found in her office desk.

Mary admired the dignified elegance of this old firehouse, its turn-of-the-century façade with three-feet-thick brick and concrete walls and two enormously majestic red doors. Inside the firehouse, she appreciated the old tin ceilings and the iron railings on the stairs leading to the second and third floors. The building was full of character, timeless and invincible. Most of all, the firehouse was starting to feel like a second home to her.

She grabbed a cup of coffee and headed to the company office. Sitting at the desk, Captain Piegere looked up at her over his reading glasses and gave her a friendly smile. She went to her private dressing area, changed into work clothes and then settled across the desk from the Captain with her coffee.

"Mary, I'm going to designate you our fire prevention Officer for Ladder 115. We give this assignment to the junior Officer in the company and it's a good way to familiarize yourself with our district and procedures.

"Currently, it's Lieutenant Murphy's job, but it appears he is to be promoted to Captain soon. While he's still here, I'm going to ask him to show you how the records are kept. We also have a training bulletin that describes the procedures step by step. As smart as you are, this will be no big challenge, but it's a necessary part of leadership for you."

She had difficulty processing what he said because she had been caught off guard hearing that Lieutenant Murphy was leaving. She was disappointed.

"Okay, Cap, sounds good," Mary replied after a quiet sigh.

She took the riding list the Captain had prepared for her and went to the apparatus floor for 6 o'clock roll call. She gave the assignments from the list to the men coming in for work. Mary introduced herself to two of the Firemen she had not met before and was happy that she remembered the names of the others.

The chauffeur, Tom Dunn, approached her.

"Lou, Ladder 115 is assigned to secure meals this month, so whenever you're ready, we can leave."

"Okay, as soon as I finish the roll call entry, we'll be off."

Later, when they arrived at the supermarket a few blocks away, four Firemen dismounted with a food list and went in to shop. Waiting in the cab, Mary shared some more easy conversation with Tom Dunn. The more time she spent with him, the better she liked and respected him.

He had four kids, a house in Smithtown, a wife, Bernadette, a second job, and totally lived for his family. Bernadette worked part-time as a school aide. Mary gathered they were a solid team. Tom's second job was at factory called Munder's Sheet Metal which was around the corner from Ladder 116, about two miles away from Ladder 115.

"Some of the guys from Ladder 116 work with me at the factory. We call ourselves "Munder's Mules.""

How familiar that name sounded, thought Mary.

"How about yourself"? Tom asked her.

Mary filled him in on single-motherhood in Levittown.

"I'm doing pretty good, cheap rent, old car, no debt, no complaints"!

The men returned for the evening meal and around 8 o'clock, everyone sat down to a delectable firehouse dinner. As Mary took her second bite of a succulent pork chop, the alarm sounded.

"Box 7251, a reported fire in a garage in back of 3920 27th Street, all units acknowledge."

"*10-4*, Ladder 115, Engine 258, Battalion 45."

As Mary hopped into the cab, her chauffer was checking the printout of assignments the housewatchman had handed him.

"Second-due, Lou."

"Okay," she replied, knowing that another ladder company would be arriving at the fire before them.

There was a lot of smoke when they arrived just west of Queens Plaza on 27th Street. Battalion 45 acknowledged to the dispatcher their arrival at the fire. The first-due adjoining company, Engine 261, already had a line stretched into the driveway and when Ladder 116 forced open the garage doors, they hit it with a heavy stream and knocked the fire down. Mary and her men checked for any extension of the fire around the perimeter of the building and all was negative.

The owner thanked the Firemen for the fast service and Ladder 115 and Engine 258 headed back to the pork chops, still scrumptious after a little warm-up. It was a quiet night for the rest of the tour.

The next morning, Mary was in the kitchen greeting some Firemen she had met already, as well as some new members. She had a system for remembering names and was mentally engaged when Tom Murphy walked in.

Again, she felt a physical reaction and made an extra effort to maintain her focus. It was not easy. When they went to their office for the relief procedures, she tried to sound nonchalant.

"Tom, I heard about your upcoming promotion to Captain. Congratulations! You must feel great."

"Hate to leave here in many ways, Lou, but, yes, I'm excited and looking forward to it."

"How long before you go"? she asked, trying not to sound more than professionally interested.

"Hopefully, next month's promotion orders. I've waited a long time," he said directly looking at Mary in a somewhat peculiar and lingering way.

Maybe it was just her imagination. But she was certainly finding it hard to break eye contact with him, "such amazing brown eyes" she thought.

Murphy gave her a little smile and turned away. Embarrassed, Mary left for her dressing area.

After quickly sprucing up and changing out of her uniform, she went to the pay phone in the hall and placed a call to Abby's apartment. Abby picked up the phone.

"Hello"?

He sounded forlorn.

"Abby, it's Mary," she announced.

Silence followed, but only momentarily and as if Mary's voice wrenched Abby from his quiet misery, he started to vent his feelings.

"Mary! My beautiful life here in America with Carol has been destroyed by my family. I am powerless to fight them. You must know that I will always love Carol and will forever regret what has happened and how much I have hurt her. My life is over"!

"I'm sorry, too. I really feel for the both of you, Abby. I know how happy you were with Carol and I can't imagine how tough it would be to have to choose between your religion and family, and the love of your life. I just wish you would have thought about that before you proposed to her and pushed to live together.

"That said, Abby, you can still call me and if I can help, I will. Rest assured, though, I will be there for Carol. Regardless of what your stubborn family thinks of her, she is a good friend and she is a a good woman."

"Yes, of all people, I know that. I would have made a different decision if only I could be assured of Carol's safety and happiness, and my own ability to stay in this country.

"Thanks for calling me, Mary. I don't know what else can be said; there is nothing that can be done to change the situation. I have already tried everything. Please pass my words to Carol. Goodbye, my friend."

CHAPTER 7

Mary reported early for her second set of day tours at Ladder 115. Her company had apparatus field inspection duty this morning from 9:30 to 1:30 p.m. Now that she was the new coordinator of building inspections for the company, she was excited about starting. Captain Piegere was in the kitchen having coffee when Mary arrived, so she poured herself a cup and joined him.

"What a gorgeous autumn day it is," Mary said to him.

"Yes, the fall leaves are beautiful in late-September. It'll be Christmas before you know it. Much traffic on your way in"? he asked.

"Not too bad, hope the rest of the day is as smooth," she answered in good spirits.

After coffee, she followed the Captain to the office.

"I've laid out the buildings to inspect. Any questions you have, Mary, I'll be glad to answer."

"Thanks, Cap."

She perused the six salmon-colored building cards and the violation checklist for all of the information she would need for their inspections.

"We haven't been in this section for two years and some of these buildings may have been demolished," advised Captain Piegere.

"It's an old factory and warehouse area. It's slated for redevelopment into a high-rise residential buildings that'll mirror the Manhattan skyline across the river. You'll find many of the buildings vacant or already demolished. Vernon Boulevard runs parallel to the East River there."

"Looks like it's going to be a ritzy area," remarked Mary.

"Yeah, very. The area runs the distance from the Midtown Tunnel to the 59ᵗʰ Street Bridge. Please note any changes you find so I can show you how to update our records."

By 9:30 a.m., Mary was on the apparatus floor assembling the men, checking the crew for neat and properly worn semi-dress uniforms. As an Officer, Mary was well aware that the importance of a professional appearance during inspections could not be overstated. Thirty minutes later, they were prepared for departure.

Because there are half the number of Ladder Companies to Engine Companies in the Department, the Ladder trucks were not used for inspections. They remained behind to respond to alarms, especially for quick search and rescue responses to fires. Some pertinent members of the two companies exchanged places with the exception of the two chauffeurs, who always were required to remain with their rigs. Mary told the chauffeur of the Engine that the rest of the team would be going to Vernon Boulevard and 46ᵗʰ Street.

"Okay, Lou, I'm Eddy Beach and I noticed your last name on the riding list. Did you have any relatives on the job"? he asked.

"My father, Gene Walsh, started as a Probie Fireman at Ladder 116 and worked there until 1967, when he was promoted to Lieutenant."

"I knew Gene. I'm on the job 30 years now. Small world. Good guy"!

"Thanks, he still misses it after retiring in '91, the same year I was appointed. I guess he passed the baton to me"! Mary joked.

"That's why I'm still here. I'm reluctant to retire"! Eddy Beach laughed.

"I actually did retire five years ago, went to Los Angeles, joined their fire department. Found out quickly it wasn't the same so I quit and re-applied for this job.

"You know, if you re-apply within a year of retirement, take the physical and pass, they'll put you back on. Best thing I ever did. Should never have left in the first place," the chauffer smiled amiably.

When they arrived at their first inspection site, the Firemen found a two-story, refrigerated warehouse building that stored frozen foods packed in the United States for shipment to Europe. Inside, there were huge freezers which were manned by a stationary refrigeration engineer, an older man Mary guessed to be about her father's age. With units this large, an engineer had to be on-site 24 hours a day. He led them to his office.

"I'm Lieutenant Walsh and we're here to inspect the premises."

"Okay, no problem," he answered.

"In addition to being the engineer, I'm also in charge of all building maintenance. My name is Vic Trnka. I'm a retired fireman, too. In fact, I went to Harry's Deli two days ago for Italian heroes and he told me that a new Lieutenant at Ladder 115 was the daughter of Gene Walsh. Harry and I both worked with your father at Ladder 116. Quite a coincidence! Anything I can do to help, you just ask."

"Thank you, Mr. Trnka"! Mary replied affably.

"I can't get over how many Firemen I have met who worked with my father. I'm thrilled to meet you guys."

"Well, Lieutenant, I can safely say that the pleasure is ours. And most of the guys have really taken to you," he stated reassuringly.

Her team's job was to inspect the entire building against the violation order checklist which consisted of labor, state and city laws pertaining to building and fire-related codes. Mary stayed with Vic to check all his permits and certificates of fitness for refrigeration. She found all licenses and permits to be in order.

Then she focused on the outside perimeter of the building; it was in immaculate shape. There was a small, well-kept lawn around the building and she noted a shed where they stored a lawnmower, a gas can and various tools for maintenance.

In the backyard facing the East River and Manhattan, she observed a table and chairs. Vic explained that the refrigeration engineers worked in 24-hour shifts and on breaks, they would relax and enjoy the passing ships and City skyline.

Sadly, Vic also informed Mary their lease was expiring next year and they were moving to make room for new land development. Vic really loved this place and took care of "his" building. When the team returned from their inspection, they, too, marveled at the orderly condition of the premises.

"You could eat off the floors, Lou," one of the men commented.

When they were leaving, Mary told Mr. Trnka that all were impressed with the way the building was maintained and no violations were found.

"When I retired from the New York City Fire Department, I went to school for stationary refrigeration engineering and have been working here for the last 15 years since. I'm heartbroken that the building will be demolished next year."

He looked crestfallen and Mary felt for him.

"Thanks for your cooperation, Mr. Trnka. I'll be sure to tell my dad about this."

"Please, call me Vic. You know I just saw Gene last year at the VA Hospital in Fort Hamilton. The Fire Department sent notices to all retirees to check for mesothelioma from chronic exposure to so much asbestos in our careers. It was like old home week! I have your father's number. I'll give him a call," Vic said and shook Mary's hand warmly.

Mary left the building and could not wait to tell her dad of yet another touching experience with a previous Fire Department Brother.

The lot next door to Vic's building was empty because the building there had already had been torn down. The next building was vacant and waiting for demolition. The next occupied building was theirs to inspect. Mary approached the front entrance and was met by a swarthy, dark-complexioned man.

"What do you want"? he asked curtly.

"We're with the New York City Fire Department. I'm Lieutenant Walsh and we're here to inspect your building."

"A woman in charge"? his voice dripping with disrespect.

Boy, not another chauvinist, Mary thought to herself.

"Yeah, she's the BOSS," one of her men piped in, reading the man's face.

The man stood blocking the entrance in a silent confrontation as Mary continued to eye him blankly in spite of her immediate distaste for him. She asked him his name and learned quickly that he was in charge of the building. She gave him the rundown of the inspection routine. He said his name was Jamal Rahman and he owned the business and rented the building. Her men took off and she asked for his licenses and permits.

"We don't use any equipment or machines that require permits," Jamal told her.

"What about your oil burner permit"?

"We only rented three months ago for one year, then the building will be brought down. I do not know where the owner keeps his permits. I do not care."

"Mr. Rahman, my men will check the oil burner and you can check your office. It may be posted. I'm going to check the outside perimeter of your building," Mary stated as she abruptly turned her back to him and walked away.

Mary took a few deep relaxation breaths and began inspecting around the decrepit old building. She wondered why in the heck anyone would rent a dump like this. In the rear yard, she was surprised to see a large mural painted on the back wall of the warehouse which faced the East River. It was a faded but still impressive panoramic scene of the Manhattan skyline and the 59th Street Bridge that crossed the river. Who knows how long it had been there, she contemplated.

She met her team at Jamal's office and was advised of the extremely poor housekeeping of the building. In addition, the aisle spaces between stocked goods were smaller than the required 36 inches and some were almost obscure and impassable.

Jamal lamely explained that most of the goods had just been moved in and that he had not had enough time to organize and arrange the stock. He produced an oil burner permit that had expired.

"Just tell the building owner to display a current permit or to renew it immediately," Mary ordered.

The Firemen made out violation reports for their findings and informed Mr. Rahman he had 15 days to comply. Jamal grunted acknowledgement and flung the orders on his desk.

Mary did not like this man. She had an ominous gut feeling about him and this warehouse.

Back in the fire truck, Fireman Albin said to Mary that he knew the man was probably a Muslim and having a woman in charge would not sit well. He lost his composure. "I can't stand these radicals ever since the terrorist bombing at the World Trade Center and the embassy bombings in Africa. Got no use for them," he declared. "My brother lost his life in the embassy bombing, sonsabitches. As far as I'm concerned, they should all just go back to their perfectly happy existence in caves and eat locusts or whatever. And we can enjoy our devilish American pork sandwiches and booze."

Albin continued on with his rant as his voiced got louder.

"Calm down, don't get emotional, Chris," Mary said, cutting him off.

CHAPTER 8

When the American pigs left on their fire truck, Jamal was a little worried he had revealed too much of his hatred toward the American Firemen. He did not want to attract attention to his mission, nor to himself, the lead operative of one of many autonomous cells placed in the United States by Osama bin Laden.

Similar clandestine cells in other areas were developing their own strikes against the American people. Jamal had learned of one cell's plan to fly commercial planes into skyscrapers after the failed World Trade Center bombing, which he thought too overreaching and complicated. He believed his operation, though much less extensive, would be equally as effective.

Three months prior to the Fire Department swine showing up, Jamal Rahman's ideas were set in motion.

He was recruiting at his mosque, carefully probing for potential jihadist. He needed men sympathetic to the injustices against the people of Islam, men who were brave and loyal in the name of Allah, men willing to die in his martyrdom operation.

Jamal had his eye on the three Hassam brothers at his mosque. The older one owned an auto repair shop in Long Island City. Jamal believed these fellow Islamic men could be useful in eventual plans.

Over the summer, he went to the shop and greeted Abdul "Abby" Hassam, the youngest, and suggested they have lunch together. They met at the Neptune Diner on 48th Street and Vernon Boulevard.

They talked about their experiences in New York since they arrived in the United States. They also talked about news from their homeland particularly of the solidarity of Egypt and Lebanon in fighting against Israel's 15-year occupation in the 'Security Zone' in southern Lebanon.

After lunch, they went outside for a smoke. Jamal asked specific questions to determine if Abby concealed any anti-American sentiment. However, Abby was not responsive to any remote suggestion of hostility toward the United States.

In fact, Abby enjoyed living in New York and seemed content with his assimilation into the American culture. He had a genuine appreciation of his new life and had been treated well by his new friends. Most of all, Abby did not believe violence resolved problems.

It was obvious, Abby was spineless coward, not a candidate for Jamal's plot. Jamal would check out Abby's two brothers, particularly Abraham, whom he had met already. While speaking with him at their mosque recently, Abraham had given Jamal the impression he held similar anti-American views.

While they were outside, Jamal looked across the street at one of the few warehouse buildings still standing in the area. He had heard that eventually all of them would be torn down. He spotted the one-story warehouse down the block that had a "for rent" sign out in front.

"May Allah protect you," Jamal said wrapping the meeting up with Abby.

Such a waste of time, he thought as he walked one block to the warehouse. It looked like a fairly new sign.

He decided to walk to the back of the building, which was on the river's edge. He looked across to the United Nations building, then looked back at the warehouse roof and then back toward the direction of Times Square in Midtown Manhattan, which he estimated was about eight or nine avenues behind the UN building.

He surveyed the surrounding area with mounting interest. It was sure to be desolate, particularly at night. Suddenly excited by his plan for attack, he roughly calculated the distance between the warehouse here in Long Island City and Times Square. Probably about four or five miles, he guessed, well within the range of Katyusha rockets and mortars.

"Allahu Akbar"! he exclaimed his hands raised beside his ears, palms up, certain that Allah has sent him this holy vision of such an attack. He return to the front of the building, memorized the realtor's number and briskly walked back to the diner to call.

"Hello, Atlas Reality, how can I help you"?

"Yes, my name is Jamal Rahman and I'm inquiring about your building for rent at 46-12 Vernon Boulevard, it's a one-story warehouse. Is it available"?

"Yes, but only for about a year. It's going to be demolished next July, as soon as they complete the landfill operation into the East River."

Yes, thought Jamal to himself, *Allah works in mysterious ways!*

"I'm interested. Can we meet"? asked Jamal.

"I'm available now," replied the agent. "My office is on Jackson Avenue, a few blocks from the warehouse."

"I'm here at the warehouse. Can you come over and show it to me"?

"Sure, I'll be there in 10 minutes," the agent said, quickly calculating the commission he would make on a building he never dreamed his agency would rent again.

Jamal was just as excited. Knowing how greedy Americans were, he would offer the American a bonus to process the paperwork promptly.

As the real estate agent pulled up to the front of the building, his excitement was slightly tempered at the sight of the dilapidated structure and he wondered who in the hell would be interested in a building like this. He got out of his car and extended his hand to Jamal, who was standing in the street waiting.

"I'm Jim Dooley. Glad to meet you."

"Yes," Jamal responded, refusing the handshake. They entered the old, rundown building and did a walk-through.

"I have a new retail supply business and need a warehouse facility right now, even if it's temporary," explained Jamal.

"If the rent is cheap enough, it will be an opportunity for me to get a jump start."

"You can have this place for a thousand a month, plus one month's security," the agent offered.

"That's a good deal. I'll take it! To be sure, Mr. Jim, if you can process the paperwork quickly, I would offer you a bonus of $200 for your trouble."

"Follow me back to the office. I'll notify the owner and draw up the lease immediately," Jim Dooley responded without hesitation.

Now, three months later, Jamal's plan had become a reality. With tutoring from a fellow Muslim who owned a wholesale company, Jamal learned how to quickly start up his own business.

He bought inventory, two used delivery vans, assembled a loyal staff, and after a short while, to his great surprise, the business was taking off and even making profits!

It was a perfect cover for his operation: an attack on Times Square on the eve of the Y2K New Year, with missiles launched from the rooftop of his Long Island City warehouse.

Since the plan's inception, he had secured two 5.2 medium-sized mortars, two rocket launchers and about 150 rounds of ammunition, some chemical, which met most of his goal of 200 rounds. The shells were smuggled into the country by his boat crew which delivered them to his warehouse under cover of night.

With exhaustive screening efforts, he had recruited 20 loyal soldiers, jihadists from area mosques who would defend the operation to their death on the night of attack. They would be well-equipped with AK-47s to protect the four crews he strategically designated to operate the mortars and rocket launchers.

His crews were comprised of his employees: four delivery drivers, two for each van to transport weapons, four warehouse workers, two each for daytime and nighttime shifts, who would operate the large weapons, and two boat men plus a bookkeeper who, including Jamal, would help transfer weapons and shells from their concealed caches stashed throughout the warehouse floor up to the roof.

His cell's team had to be legal residents in the United States. He wanted no problems with Immigration or any agency that could blow their cover. Cell phone communication was strictly prohibited.

Training over the next six-months would be well-coordinated and intense. He believed that Allah would guide him.

And as the months passed, Jamal's faith in his plan of attack grew.

CHAPTER 9

A month had gone by and Mary was starting to feel confident in her new position at the Fire Department. She knew the attitudes toward women in the department prevailed, but so far, everything had been copacetic at her house. She also believed that some of the senior men who knew her father were contributory toward her being accepted, and she would not disappoint them.

Tom Murphy was coming up for promotion in a few days. Mary grew used to her crush on him. She found out he was single, no children, was in a marriage that sadly ended with his wife's death two years ago from breast cancer. Mary's subtle inquiries revealed how devastated he had been after her death and how, just lately, he seemed to be getting past the grieving phase.

Mary had taken over the fire prevention job and found it quite interesting, but very time-consuming if all records were kept updated and orderly. It also gave her a small jolt of satisfaction, knowing that most male Lieutenants hated the job.

Tomorrow was re-inspection duty for the violation orders served last month. She couldn't wait until she had another look at that obnoxious occupant two doors away from Vic Trnka's warehouse. She called and he picked up the phone.

"Hi, Mr. Trnka, it's Mary Walsh from the firehouse. I have re-inspections this morning and I was hoping I'd catch you at work today to visit with you."

"Love to see you, Mary. I'll be here all day, but please call me Vic, okay"? he insisted.

When the apparatus pulled up to Vic's place, he was outside sweeping the sidewalk. He sure looked like he was going to miss the place. Seeing the fire truck and the Brothers made him smile; the Firemen equally appreciated their visit with Vic, a throwback to the "old school," who they held in high regard.

He invited everyone in for coffee, remembering all too well how many gallons were consumed on an average day at the old firehouse. Afterward, Mary wanted a few words with Vic in private. She asked her men to wait out back. It was a beautiful day and her guys would enjoy the waterfront and spectacular view of the City.

"Vic, I just wanted to ask you about that man who rented the warehouse two doors down. I can't get over this creepy feeling I have about him. He has some real hostile vibes," Mary confided.

Vic nodded in affirmation.

"Yep. I've seen a lot of activity over there, Lou. They've built a canopy of some sort on the roof. In fact, I went up to my roof, which is a story higher, and I can see it's a metal-framed structure that looks like a big bus stop.

"Some of the men were up there eating their lunch. I also noticed some rugs on the roof, which I guess they use for praying. I assume they're Muslim. I introduced myself to the owner one day, tried to start up a conversation, but he was very aloof, not very friendly at all," Vic divulged to Mary.

"Okay, thanks, Vic, I was just wondering, we're heading over there next."

She thanked Vic and said goodbye, collected her men, then drove to the front of Jamal's building.

When she knocked at the door, the man she had met before, opened the door. Mary was immediately taken aback by his friendly demeanor.

"Hello, Lieutenant, the place is ready for your visit. I spoke to the owner and he gave me the oil burner permit," he smiled as he handed it to Mary.

"I also cleaned up the place and complied with the orders from your Fire Department."

"Okay, good," she replied, wary of Jamal Rahman's abrupt change in personality.

"My men will do a walk-through and check. It's required."

She stayed with Jamal while the men re-inspected the violations. She was taken off-guard by his accommodating behavior and kept her distance. When the men returned, they informed her that the place was much improved and cleaned up. The aisle space and door accesses were clear.

Mary spotted the new stairway to the roof and the modified opening which was enlarged. She pointed to the area.

"You've changed the scuttle opening to the roof, I see."

"Yes, I have," answered Jamal.

"The old iron ladder to the small roof opening was very dangerous for my men. We use the roof frequently for *salat*, our daily prayers to Allah. On nice days, we take our lunch break up there."

Mary noted their rugs and folding chairs and tables stored next to the staircase.

"I would like to evaluate the roof, please."

"Of course," answered Jamal.

"The owner has obtained the necessary temporary permits for the work."

Up on the roof, Mary observed the structure Vic spoke of. It stretched to almost the width of the roof. It looked like a big bus stop, as Vic described, with an overhang of about 20 feet, or more like a band shell, Mary thought. It was built of plastic ribbed roofing sections screwed into a lightweight metal frame. The sheets were semi-translucent allowing light in while affording protection from inclement weather.

"If you have any questions, I can call the owner now and you can speak to him," Jamal offered, breaking Mary's concentration.

"That would be good," Mary said.

Jamal left to make the phone call from his office with Mary following close behind. He dialed and when the landlord answered, Jamal handed her the phone.

"The owner's name is Joshua Levine."

"Mr. Levine, Lieutenant Mary Walsh here, from the New York City Fire Department. I would like to know about the work permits you have for the roof construction."

"Yes, Lieutenant. I have temporary permits from the Buildings Department. The actual permits are forthcoming. The building inspectors approved the construction and the changes my tenant wanted to make to the roof.

"It didn't affect the building structure, only widened the roof access to make it easier to get to the roof. I'm sure you are aware that this building is scheduled for demolition next July"? Mr. Levine emphasized.

"Yes, I am," replied Mary.

"When the permits arrive, give them to your tenant so they can be displayed on premises, okay"?

"Will do, that's no problem. As soon as I receive them, I'll get them to Jamal."

Mary handed the phone back to Jamal.

"Everything appears to be in order. Thanks for your cooperation, Mr. Rahman."

"Anything I can do to help, thank you, Lieutenant," he answered cordially as he walked Mary to the door.

When the Firemen left, Jamal was consumed with anger but he was glad there were no further problems with the warehouse.

"*Soon they will see,*" he seethed.

The rest of the morning, she and the men revisited other re-inspections which were minor in nature. As the men worked, she ruminated over Jamal. What an *about-face* she thought. She commented to the men on Mr. Rahman's sudden personality switch.

"I think it's a bullshit act," Fireman Drake acknowledged.

"I saw some of his employees speaking in their own language and looking at us, and their expressions were anything but friendly. I don't trust them," he added.

Mary digested this a few moments.

"We're done here"! she announced. "Let's head back to the firehouse. It's lunch time"!

Mary gave up on finding a reasonable explanation for Jamal's odd behavior.

Still, the ominous feeling in her gut remained.

CHAPTER 10

It was mid-October and Jamal Rahman was on the roof of his warehouse. It was a cool, calm evening and he was savoring the view of the expansive Manhattan skyline. The inverted reflection of the illuminated City was crystal clear on the East River.

He often would come here by himself when the business day was over. He used the peace and quiet to evaluate his progress and to smooth out any logistical crimps in his operation.

His wholesale business, selling cheap items to flea markets, street vendors and ninety-nine-cent stores, was doing extremely well. Artificial flowers were his best item, along with Christmas decorations, cheap electronics, watches and the like.

At times inconvenient but essential to the success of his attack plan, Jamal had to legitimize his cover wholesale business. Permits, sales tax, payrolls, social security and unemployment contributions all had to be recorded correctly. Shadeed Cromitie, his CPA who he recruited from his mosque, oversaw all the record-keeping and requirements necessary to run the business.

Jamal's estimated attack force included at least 35 people now, some of which were known al Qaeda operatives experienced and trained in terrorist camps overseas. The newer recruits were cautiously screened for their loyalty to the cell and their commitment to the Y2K martyrdom mission.

Jamal had despised Americans for as long as he could remember. He felt the country supported the suppression of Muslims all over the world. Unlike Abby, who was weak and peace-loving, Abby's brother, Abraham, was a perfect candidate for his mission.

However, with Abraham's illegal status, his student visa long since expired, Jamal could only enlist him for the day of attack as part of the defense force. But since Abraham was also an expert mechanic, he possibly could be useful in other ways, Jamal surmised as a chilly wind cut through him.

Despite his operation's reassuring progress, his sense of security was dissipating and he was paranoid about his cell being discovered the closer Y2K approached. Too many terrorist organizations had been infiltrated by the FBI, he feared. This meant he could trust only a few of only his most loyal soldiers with exact details of the operation.

Accordingly, each of the 20 defense soldiers would only receive their weapons--AK-47s and Glock automatic pistols--on New Year's Eve. The firearms, supplied with Jamal's money, would be procured in the underground markets which meant the sales were facilitated with no questions asked. Weapons' dealers in the black market were greedy enough, and well-known among drug cartels, terrorist groups, thieves and street gangs.

His plan was to deploy the soldiers to the warehouse on the night of the attack to rebuff any attempts to thwart the attack on Times Square. The soldiers would man stations guarding the roof, windows and doors, keeping the infidels at bay during the midnight offensive.

He employed the same surreptitious tactics to maintain secrecy by mandating legal immigration status for his warehouse employees due to the potential for unexpected visits from the Immigration and Naturalization Service. Only a handful of loyal followers were selected to help conceal the larger weapons and ammunition. These men were trained weapons operators and needed for the night of the attack.

He had in his possession at the warehouse two dismantled mortars, light at 90 pounds, with a range of five to six miles. Also included were two dismantled Katyusha rocket launchers, lighter than the mortars, but with a range of 12 miles. He especially liked these, as they could be used to deliver chemical shells. And his stockpile of anti-personnel weaponry was already two-thirds complete.

The ultimate goal of Jamal's attack with these anti-personnel weapons was to create mass hysteria in Times Square among the revelers celebrating the Y2K New Year. Jamal thought himself very clever to piggy-back his attack on the media's alarming "Millennium Bug" hype which predicted that computer mainframes would crash when the year passed from 1999 to 2000. Pandemonium would reverberate throughout New York City sparking potential for catastrophic panic, shutting down businesses, utilities and markets in the United States, which would affect the economy worldwide.

The abundance of artificial flowers Jamal had stored in the factory came in very handy to obscure his powerful tools of terror. He had about 150 shells which his men would assemble and arm on the roof shortly before the launch of the salvos into Times Square. He was hoping to add 50 more shells to his arsenal from the sympathetic nations with ships importing legitimate cargo to the New York ports.

Maintaining holding patterns off of Long Island, ships lined up all the way to the Verrazano Bridge area in Brooklyn awaiting turns to unload their cargo when dock space became available. This process usually took days.

Almahdi "Ali" Hussein, one of Jamal's most loyal and talented operatives, owned a 30-foot, medium-sized fishing boat that he docked at one of the Sheepshead Bay public fishing facilities in Brooklyn. Scanning shipping trade news posts and Coast Guard publications, Ali followed the tightly accurate schedules of the freighters. Knowing the date and time of arrival, Ali would contact an on-board accomplice and get the ship's exact location in the holding pattern.

He would leave Sheepshead Bay with his trusted first mate, Samir "Sammy," for a supposed night of fishing. Ali and Sammy would position the boat near the designated ship usually when it was closest to the Coney Island area, and begin fishing. Flashlight signals between the freighter and the fishing boat indicated when it was safe to begin the weapons transfer.

The rendezvous area was at the ship's lower hold access door facing away from the shoreline. Nights with too much moonlight and clear visibility were avoided and contingency plans would be made for another night when the ship moved along the line. This would bring the boat closer to New York Harbor where extreme caution was taken to remain undetected by local authorities.

When contact was made, the cache of weapons was transferred to wooden boxes holding four shells each and lowered by rope to the fishing boat. The rope then was tied to the rails and the boxes were slipped a few feet below water level. The weapons could easily be mistaken for bait boxes. Deliveries were always small, allowing the weapons to be hidden aboard the ships and Ali's small boat would have adequate control of the illicit cargo.

Ali knew the tides and would bring his boat to the mouth of the East River. Ali and Sammy would fish until the incoming tide would make their upstream delivery to the warehouse easier. Ali then would proceed to the deserted bulkhead in back of Jamal's building.

One night, a police car was parked in the vacant lot next to the warehouse when he and Sammy pulled near the bulkhead. One of the cops got out of his patrol car, walked to the bulkhead and wanted to know what Ali and Sammy were fishing for.

Ali quickly replied that sea bass and other fish in the area were plentiful.

"Are they safe to eat? Isn't the water polluted"? asked the curious officer.

Ali, an experienced fisherman, was knowledgeable about New York's Clean Water Act of the '70s.

"Yes, since the City's cleaned up the water, fish have returned to the river. The fishing's great now"! he reassured the officer.

"Good luck," the cop replied, not particularly interested, and returned to his car.

The men waited until the police finally left to complete their delivery to the back door of the warehouse where the two night men were anxiously awaiting. The four, following Jamal's strict instructions, now hid the cargo in various places within the warehouse.

Jamal keenly evaluated other avenues for transporting weapons to the warehouse. Abraham explained to Jamal the possibilities of hiding ammunition shells in the hollow tubes that held the drive shafts of the two delivery vans. Once the drive shaft was lowered by removing the bolts, it could be removed from the hollow tube. The hollow space then could be used to smuggle small missiles and weapons parts.

"I've heard this is a way dealers move their drugs," said Abraham.

Jamal was impressed.

"It sounds like a good plan. We will keep it in mind in case we need more ammunition."

Finally, near midnight, his pack of cigarettes gone, Jamal went down the stairs to the warehouse. His two night security men were on the job and alert. They were needed for surveillance and to receive Ali's fishing boat deliveries.

"May Allah reward you for the good," he wished them, and left.

Since it was within a short walking distance to the Flushing #7 subway line at Vernon and Jackson Boulevards, he set off at a brisk pace. There, he took the train to his apartment in Manhattan. Tomorrow would be another busy day, he anticipated. He would need a good night's sleep.

CHAPTER 11

Tom Murphy was promoted to Captain on the October orders and the firehouse started planning a promotion party at Harry's place. Harry was ecstatic when he learned about the event. The crew planned the celebration for Friday night and Mary was happy the men had gone out of their way and invited her.

After touching base with Sheila, Mary decided to stay overnight at the firehouse since she was scheduled to work day shifts Friday and Saturday. Having her own bunk room meant there would be no problem staying over. Being the only woman in the firehouse did have some advantages.

At Harry's, in addition to the bocce court in the rear yard, there was a small bar with an overhang in case it rained. In the space between Harry's Deli and the outside courtyard, there was a shuffleboard court and tables and chairs for card playing. This was where the food was set up the night of the party. Harry's assortment of meatballs, sausage and peppers, roasted meats and his pot roast and noodles was strictly gourmet.

It turned out to be a great party. Firemen who had been promoted from other firehouses in the Battalion also shared the celebration with Captain Murphy, as was usually the case with promotion parties. There were a lot of new and old faces. Many introductions were made and many war stories shared. Firemen love to rag on each other with all of their embarrassing encounters. It was a night of warm friendships and revelry. Drinks flowed and the laughing got louder.

Vic Trnka and a few old buddies from her dad's era had also been invited. Harry was among them laughing it up, when Vic saw Mary and said to Harry.

'Have you met Gene Walsh's daughter, Mary? She's the new Lieutenant at Ladder 115."

"I've seen her, but was never introduced". He extended his hand and Mary clasped Harry's huge hand and felt the strength that her father had described about him.

Her dad had been part of Harry's personal kitchen staff which did the shopping of the food, doing his directed culinary small jobs such as peeling potatoes, chopping vegetables and doing the after dinner dish washing. Harry also had an array of iron pots and pans and there was hell to pay if they were ever touched and cleaned with dish detergents. They had to be wiped out with brown paper towels and olive oil.

Harry also simonized cars when he was off-duty to pay his gambling debts since his bookies were not exactly patient with late payments. He also would polish the aerial ladder truck from front to rear, keeping it sparkling. This is what legends are made of particularly to newly assigned probationary firemen.

Harry Galleo, originally, Aneillo Galiotfiore, was born in Italy and still to this day had a slight accent. He came to America just before World War II, he joined the army to fight for the country he knew would become his own and thus became a U.S. Citizen. After the war, he took the test for the Fire Department and was appointed in the late forties. He put 35 years in the Department and any man who worked alongside him never forgot the experience.

The party was turning into old home week for the veteran Firemen. It was also a wonderful introduction for the new Firemen. It allowed them to witness the dedication, love and tribute to an everlasting Brotherhood of Firemen. Similar to that of a close, active military unit, these men placed service to their country and community above their own safety and security. Every day, they worked together as a team to face danger in order to save the lives of fellow Americans.

One man out of Harry's group approached Mary.

"Hi, I'm Roy Teverbaugh. Your father and I both worked together as firemen," He extended his hand and Mary searched her memory for the name. It sounded so familiar. Finally, it came to her.

"I know your name. Dad used to tell me the story of your key role in the Van Iderstine fire."

Van Iderstine was a factory in Long Island City where animal fat was used to make soap and glue. In the early days, any animal that died on the streets of New York, such as wagon horses, circus animals even as large as elephants that died when the circus came to town, were taken to the Van Iderstine Factory. The animals were put into a giant funnel machine with meat grinders at the bottom that ground up their bodies. These now smaller more manageable pieces were brought to other buildings on the large factory premises where the fat was rendered to make soap and glue. Van Iderstine trucks also would go to butcher shops all over the City to buy waste fat and bones

The factory had five buildings that were all part of the plant. Because of the nature of their business, there was grease everywhere, which caused many fires. Some of these fires were small and others were very large and dangerous. In December of 1964, six Firemen were killed when a heavy roof in one of the buildings collapsed on top of them.

Mary's dad used to tell her about another large fire at the Van Iderstine Factory, when Roy Teverbaugh's Engine 261 came back to quarters with all its hoses draped every which way over the apparatus. The hoses were so loaded with grease that they slipped from the hands of the Firemen, preventing them from orderly packing the hose in the hose bed.

The Firemen wound up closing off the block and laid out the hose in front of the firehouse to try and clean it with brushes, soap and water. It was not effective. This is when Roy came up with his clever idea.

He suggested employing the same process they used to make foam for extinguishing oil fires. However, rather than using a foam solution, they would use a big can of industrial detergent to make suds instead.

It worked, and with a large detergent blanket of bubbles and water, the Firemen scrubbed the hoses with large straw brooms. Other fire hoses connected to hydrants were used to rinse away the suds. As a result, the hoses turned out cleaner than ever.

"My father was so impressed with the operation and your ingenuity, he told me the story many times throughout the years. Unforgettable"! exclaimed Mary.

Roy laughed and Mary could see how pleased he was that she knew the story. Mary was glad her father was such a great storyteller.

After a night of comradely cheer, it was getting late and time to head back to the firehouse, which was walking distance away. Mary was walking with a small group of Firemen and Tom caught up with them.

"I have a few last-minute things to pick up and then I'm yesterday's news. You guys won't even miss me," he said facetiously. A negative response followed and Tom laughed. "You better not forget me".

The Firemen continued to maintain stoic expressions, playing along, until finally they could hold out no longer and everybody burst out laughing, giving their leader and friend hearty pats on the back.

A covering Lieutenant in Ladder 115 was in the kitchen when they arrived and the group sat together for quite a while. As an extension of the party, the Firemen continued to exchange old stories and jobs that were brought up earlier. Reminiscing was something of which they never tired.

"My pillow is waiting and tomorrow will come fast, so goodnight and thanks, guys,"

Mary finally said.

In the office, she sat thinking about the exciting night, when Tom walked in. He picked up his clothes and toiletries for the "bag" he soon would be carrying again to various firehouses until his permanent firehouse was assigned.

When he finished packing, Tom reached out and took Mary's hand in both of his. There was an awkward silence.

"Mary, it's been great working with you." He stopped for a moment, looking away, while still holding her hand.

He looked back into her eyes.

"As your supervisor, ethically, I was restricted from sharing my personal thoughts about you. Don't mistake that for lack of interest," he smiled awkwardly.

"It's been there the whole time -- my attraction to you, that is -- and I hope you won't find me too forward, but I'd like to see you again. Any chance I can get your number"? he asked, hoping Mary would not refuse.

Mary had to pause to stymie her excitement.

"I would really like that," she responded casually.

They exchanged numbers and kissed each other lightly on the cheeks, saying goodbye as Tom walked out the door.

Mary had a feeling something significant had just happened, and she predicted her life was going to change. With a little buzz on, she danced and hummed in her bunk room and didn't care if anyone noticed.

Tom floated down the stairs from the company office, elated that Mary had given him her phone number. Entering the kitchen on the second floor, Tom was surprised to see how many members had come back to the firehouse from the party. They all congratulated him again on his promotion to Captain. He was well-liked and a very efficient Officer. He would be missed.

Tom said goodnight and headed for his car which he parked in front of quarters. He had very little to drink at the party because of his drive home to Ridgewood, Queens, where he had lived with his wife, Fran.

Two years had passed since Fran's death from breast cancer and he pondered how he would feel dating someone for the first time. He would never forget Fran and only wished they had had children to keep a part of her with him.

The first year after Fran's death, Tom studied for Captain obsessively and the required intensity helped him dilute the pain of losing her. He took the Captain's test, did well and hit the top of the list.

Before Fran died, he loved playing golf -- once a week with his firehouse buddies and once a week at the Forest Park Golf Course with Fran, who also loved the game. At that time, he was a Fireman at Ladder 135 on Myrtle Avenue in Ridgewood, which was a predominately German neighborhood.

After golf, he and Fran would go to Zum Stammitsch, a well-known German restaurant, to drink German beer from their tall thin Pilsner glasses and eat a late lunch, usually their favorite knockwurst or bratwurst with sauerkraut. It was at this restaurant that they had first met.

Fran was a part-time waitress there while she was an English major at New York University. Tom had wound up at Zum Stammitsch with his buddies after a long day of golfing.

Tom and Fran fell in love after dating a short while, and when she graduated college, they got married and bought a house three blocks away from Zum Stammitsch. After graduation, Fran interned at Macmillan Publishing in Manhattan, which she hoped would lead her into a writing career. They were very happy with each other and then Fran got sick and Tom's world fell apart.

CHAPTER 12

Mary washed the evening dinner dishes with Toni-Ann. After the kitchen was cleaned up, she went out to the picnic table and lit up a cigarette.

God, she hated this habit, she thought to herself. She was going to have to quit for Toni-Ann's sake, if nothing else. She thought of her daughter lovingly.

"It's a free night for us, Sweetheart!" she called in to Toni Ann.

"I've got us a movie, *it's Free Willy*, and we've got popcorn and ice cream, too, so go do your homework and we'll get started, okey-dokey"?

"Yippee"! Toni-Ann squealed with delight and ran to her room.

The phone rang, Mary picked it up and said hello, but there was no response.

"Hello, hello"? Mary repeated annoyed.

When she was just about to hang up, she heard a subdued voice and instantly recognized it as Abby's.

"I know you must hate me for what my family did to Carol," he burst out, pausing for Mary's response.

Mary said nothing and waited for him to continue.

"I was treated so kindly by you and everybody and, particularly because of this, it must seem like a real stab in the back to you and Carol and Carol's family and your father. Does your father hate me"? Abby asked worriedly.

"Well, Abby, he's not very pleased with you right now and I'm not either. I just think your loyalties should have been to your so-called loving partner," Mary said sternly.

Abby sighed.

"I know. I'm so filled with disgust for myself, but I can't break away from my family and my religion. I tried.

"I wanted you to know, I have a new mechanic's job in a garage not far from the one we owned. I'm saving money so I can return to Lebanon, probably early next year. I would like to meet with you and get some feedback before I go. Would that be okay"? Abby asked.

Mary always liked Abby, so it was easy to put her anger aside.

"Okay. Let's see. I'm working days Thursday and Friday, so we could possibly meet on either day after my tour," she offered.

"Any day is okay with me. Abby said.

How does Thursday night at 7 o'clock sound, after I get off work? Where should we meet? Asked Mary.

Abby took a moment to consider a good place.

"There's that Diner on 48th Street and Vernon Boulevard, Is that good"?

"That's fine. I know where it is. See you there, Abby."

As Mary hung up the phone, she wondered what he wanted to talk about. He obviously made up his mind to leave America for Lebanon, so she was surprised he would seek her counsel. Hearing Toni finishing up with her homework, she quickly dismissed the thought.

On Thursday evening Mary drove to the diner, remembering its location from previous inspection visits and arrived before Abby. Pulling into the parking space, she noticed some tables and chairs outside and, though it was autumn, she thought it might still be comfortable enough to sit outside. She chose a table that enabled her to look across the river to Manhattan.

She was glad that many of the old factory and warehouse buildings on the river's edge had been torn down. Directly across the river stood the U.N. complex. She ordered coffee, lit a cigarette and enjoyed the view while she waited for Abby.

He arrived not too long afterward and Mary, spotting him, did a double take. To her surprise, Abby had grown a beard which thoroughly changed his handsome, clean-shaven appearance. He really looked like a Muslim now.

Abby grasped her hand and sat down. She noticed the wistful look in his eyes.

"Thanks for coming, Mary. I have to talk to someone I trust. I feel so alone, with nowhere to turn. It is a dead-end road for me here."

Mary felt sorry for him despite what had happened, they did share many good times together.

"My life as I know it, is over. Being with Carol was the happiest part of my life. She loved me and I was treated with kindness and respect by her and her friends and family. Now, I wind up not giving anything in return, except hurt and pain," Abby confessed.

"Abby, you tried, we all love you and enjoy being with you. Never forget that. But we're all left with the same foregone conclusion. Your family's strong beliefs present an insurmountable barrier to your relationship with Carol. It's just the way it is. I hope you recover from this sad situation, too," Mary offered.

"I'll never meet anyone like Carol. Sometimes, I wish that I had been born and raised in America. It would have made this so much less complicated," he looked out at the river.

They both sat there without speaking for a while. Mary sensed that Abby wanted to stay and talk. The waiter came over with menus and asked if they would like anything to drink.

"Mary, would you like a glass of wine"? Abby asked her.

"Sure, I'll have a glass of red wine, please," Mary smiled at the waiter.

Abby requested iced tea.

Mary realized drinking alcohol was generally forbidden among Muslims, but in the past, Abby drank beer, and lots of it. In fact, he always seemed to have a Heineken in his hand anytime Mary saw him. Apparently, he also had to give this up, she thought.

Looking for something to talk about, Mary pointed to the two isolated buildings on 46th Street.

"I was on inspection duty last month and those were my first two buildings."

Abby was startled, but said nothing, knowing that Jamal had rented the smaller building and his brother, Abraham, was involved with him on some secret project.

"The smaller building was rented to a guy and I didn't like him. I hate to say this, but I think he's a Muslim, too. He was so arrogant to me and my men and uncooperative-- his employees weren't any better," Mary told Abby.

"You know from my family's actions with Carol what some of my people are like. I wish it could be different. The Jewish problems with the Palestinians and Lebanese people are not good. Most of my people view Israel as an aggressive occupier. They also think it is American politics that support the Israeli government. I'm not saying that I agree completely, I love this place, but as a Muslim, I can see both sides," Abby explained.

Mary nodded her head, without sharing her opinion. She decided it would be prudent to say no more on this complex issue. Fortunately, the waiter returned for their food order. Mary ordered a salad with grilled chicken.

"I'll have the same," Abby said.

While they were eating, Mary and Abby kept the conversation light. Mary shared some of her latest job experiences in her new firehouse. Abby enjoyed her stories and even laughed a little. The evening suddenly became quite chilly as they finished and Abby told Mary he would go inside and pay the check. Afterward, he walked her to her car and asked if he could see her again sometime.

"I'm stuck between two cultures with no way out, Mary. I would appreciate having someone to talk to."

"Okay by me, Abby. Our jobs are close and we can get together now and then. Just give me a call."

They gave each other a light hug, as they always had.

As he left, Mary watched him walk away, his shoulder slumped. All she could do was focus on his bright green and white Jets jacket. What a contradiction, she thought. He was a huge Jets fan and followed them through every football season.

She sadly thought how his dreams of living in America had been squashed by his family. She was hit with a wave of profound sadness as the story, *A Man Without a Country*, came to mind.

CHAPTER 13

After finishing up two night tours, Mary had 72 hours off. Finally, she would have a Friday night for herself to go dancing with her girlfriends. Mary loved to get dressed up in one of her short, slinky dresses and wear sexy makeup and jewelry.

Her friends all agreed Mary looked hot when she got dressed up. It was such a departure from her manly work clothes. She and Carol and Carol's sister, Barbara, and their friend, April, were going dancing at Zachary's in East Meadow, one of the many late-night dance clubs on Long Island with great DJs.

This night out was also a much-needed break for Carol. At first, she had been reluctant when it was suggested it might get her out of her doldrums, so Mary had their mutual friend, April, who could be very persuasive, call and convince her.

April was a beautiful Maltese woman they had befriended years ago. She lived next to Long Beach, in Island Park, so she told Carol that she would drive her and Barbara to the club.

Mary would meet all of them at Zachary's. She liked to have her car in case a call came in with an emergency concerning Toni-Ann.

At Zachary's, they were dancing up a storm, having a ball, when April's ex-boyfriend, Assad, a friend of Abby's, arrived. April had broken off with him not too long ago because of his insane jealousy issues and, for months now, he had been trying to convince her to come back to him.

Tonight, April would have no part of it. When Assad tried to talk to her, she called him a creep and told him to get lost. April was no pushover and she had had it with Assad at this point. After the humiliating public rejection, Assad became intensely angry and started yelling at her, his face in hers.

Carol intervened trying to calm him down.

"Assad, please, I'm begging you, this is not a good time nor place to talk to her. She is angry and you are very upset."

"You're right, Carol. I'll leave," he said and stormed out of the dance club.

The girls thought nothing about it because Assad had been irate and dramatic like that in the past. So the girls resumed dancing the night away and soon forgot the incident.

It was two in the morning when the girls left Zachary's and walked Mary to her car in the parking lot.

"I had such a fantastic time, as always. I'll be in touch. We'll do it again soon"! Mary said and after goodbye hugs, she got into her car.

Driving to Long Beach, April, Carol and Barbara stopped off at the White Castle drive-thru on Sunrise Highway. They ordered hamburgers, fries, milk shakes then continued on to Carol's mother's to eat. There, they replayed the night's adventures in between mouthfuls of infamous White Castle *belly-bombers.*

They had all spotted good-looking men and schmoozed and danced with a few.

"Any keepers"? asked Barbara.

"Maybe. We'll just have to go back out again," grinned April.

"Too bad Assad showed up," Barbara frowned.

"That's okay. I'm just glad he's out of my life. I couldn't take how possessive he was, always asking who I was with and where I was going. It might be okay for their women, not for me"! April exclaimed looking at her watch.

"Wow, it's so late! I gotta go, call you gals later"! April gushed, and out the door she left.

Very early the next day, the phone rang. Mary groaned and got out of bed to answer. Just when she could stay in bed, she thought.

The call was from Sheila, who was in a very agitated state.

"Are you okay, Mary"?

"Yes, what's wrong? Is something wrong with Toni-Ann"? Mary asked suddenly panic-stricken.

"No, no, Toni-Ann is fine. Oh, it's just terrible. They announced on the radio that there was a girl murdered in Island Park early this morning by a jealous boyfriend. They didn't give any names or addresses, but I thought about your friend, April. I know she has a crazy Muslim boyfriend."

"Sheila, I'll call you back. I have to call Carol. I'll keep you posted with any news," Mary said fully awake now.

Mary's hands trembled as she called Carol's house. Ellen, Carol's mother, answered after only one ring.

"Hi, it's Mary. I just got a strange call about a girl murdered in…"

Ellen quickly interrupted.

"It's April and we're just getting the news, too. Carol's hysterical. We can't believe it"! Ellen said, beside herself with shock.

She told Mary how April had just left her house early this morning.

"The whole story's not in yet, but they said Assad was found walking around in a daze near his home and when the cops picked him up, he confessed to stabbing April. He must have been waiting for her when she got home."

"Oh, my God! How did he get into her house"? Mary questioned.

"He probably never returned his key and April would never have thought to change the locks."

"Tell Carol I'll call her right back," said Mary.

"Okay, Mary, she's on the other line with Barbara now," answered her mother.

Mary hung up, so upset; she couldn't think straight and just sat immobilized on the side of her bed. She tried to get her thoughts in order. How could this have happened? What should we have done differently last night? What could we have done?

Mary's thoughts raced and raced. What the hell is going on lately? First, there's the incident with Carol and Abby's family, now this! Not to mentioned that jack-ass factory guy. All this crazy radical behavior!

Mary called Sheila back to let her know it was true, Assad had killed April.

"Mary, I'll keep Toni-Ann the rest of the day. There's going to be a lot going on with you and everyone. I'll bring the girls back tonight," Sheila offered. "No, it's alright, I think I could use company, can you come over with the girls for awhile?"

"Yes, I'll even pick up some bagels, the girls haven't eaten yet."

Sheila arrived shortly with the girls and two big bags of assorted bagels and various cream cheese spreads, bought from their favorite bagel store in Levittown. Mary was relieved to see Sheila and the happy faces of the girls searching through the bagel bag. Company is what Mary needed right now. The easy banter among them kept Mary from thinking about April and the unbelievable tragedy.

After breakfast the girls wanted to play in the backyard, the day was sunny and warm, so they took their dolls to play house. Mary offered another cup of coffee to Sheila. "Yes, I would like another cup, to help wash down the two bagels I just ate! They are so delicious with these spreads."

"Yes, they are but, I'm afraid I don't have much of an appetite."

"Are you alright, Mary?"

"I feel numb", replied Mary. "I still can't believe it's happened, it's surreal, this happens to other people not to someone you know!"

Sheila listened as her friend told what she knew of the story, breaking down into sobs. "I feel so helpless!" Sheila put her arms around Mary to try and comfort her. They jumped apart as the girls ran in from outside.

"We want to watch television now. We're thirsty, is there any soda Mom?"

"Yes, in the fridge, and here are some M&M's you girls can have." Replied Mary as they squealed with delight. Mary was happy to have the girls in the house.

"How about I keep the girls here for the night since you have to work in the morning Sheila, it would save you a trip and I could use the company."

"That would be fine, Mary, in fact I have some errands to run so I think I'll leave soon."

Mary spent the day with the girls, watching TV with them, a movie and playing two board games. Early evening they went out for pizza with Sheila joining them at the pizza parlor.

"Would you like to come back to the house for a few beers, Sheila?"

"Sounds good, just for a little while since I have to get up early."

After a couple of TV shows the girls were put to bed and Sheila left. Mary decided to call her Dad. She had called him and Elizabeth earlier in the morning to tell them what happened. Neither was surprised at the irrational behavior of Assad. Now Mary's Dad answered the phone.

"Hi Mary, I've been waiting for your call. You don't have to talk about it, the details have been on the News. How are you holding up?" Her father asked, concerned.

"I'm so pissed off, Dad! What's wrong with these people"? Mary vented.

"This is not normal behavior, Dad. Look at how Abby's family treated Carol. In fact, I'd like you to talk to Carol, especially now, Dad. I think Abby and his brothers should be reported and checked out."

Gene thought about his suggestion for a moment realizing his daughter's concern.

"O.K. Mary, you can talk to Carol and tell her to come over when she's ready, perhaps when things settle down a bit. We'll sort things out," he reassured.

"Great, Dad, thanks. I'm exhausted now and emotionally spent. I'll talk to Carol and I'll let you know more about what's going on. I love you Dad."

She hung up the phone, and headed to bed.

---⟨✳⟩---

CHAPTER 14

Mary called Carol the next morning before Toni-Ann was awake and told her about the conversation with her dad.

"Carol, we all know Abby is pretty incapable of violence, but his brothers, Abraham and Mohammed, are a totally different story. They despise us and our culture. The way Abby's family treated you was way too extreme and potentially dangerous. At this point, I think we're obligated to report Abby and Abraham to Immigration. Their student visas have been expired for a long time. They do not accept our way of life; do not like us, so why should they still be in our country? I know how Abby is and we all liked him, he loved this country and our way of living but his family will not tolerate that and their actions along with what happened to April should be a message to us."

"I agree, Mary, and if I can just collect my thoughts and settle down, I will call your father and get some advice from him and Elizabeth," Carol promised.

They talked some more and hung up. Mary's next call was to her father. She asked if she could come over.

"Sure, Mary, come on over. I'll be home all day." He said; looking forward to seeing his daughter.

When she got there, she told her dad and Elizabeth about the conversation she had with Carol and that Carol will be calling them for advice on how to report Abby and his brothers, to the authorities.

"We'll be waiting for her call. Now, how about you and I take a nice walk on the boardwalk and spend a little time together on this beautiful, sunny day"?

"That would be great, Dad. I need that."

They spent a few hours walking the two-and-a-quarter-mile boardwalk. Conversation was always easy between them. While enjoying the sun and walking the boardwalk, they stopped to rest at one of the benches that faced the Atlantic Ocean. Many of them had small memorial plaques affixed to them in honor of Long Beach residents. At the end of the boardwalk, they stopped at Vito's for pizza and beer.

"Boy, Dad, I needed a fix like this"!

"So did I, Mary," he smiled back.

Mary was so happy for her dad, particularly with his marriage to Elizabeth. He met her 20 years ago when she had come to her dad's firehouse on 85th Street in Manhattan. He was Captain at Ladder 13 back then.

Remarkably, Elizabeth was an ex-nun who left the order after five years to become an FBI agent. Three years in the Bureau, she was assigned to an arson investigation involving a high-rise residential management company. The company was suspected of hiring an arsonist to set fires to several of the City's old walk-up tenements so they could be replaced with luxury apartment buildings.

It became a famous case. After that, they fell in love and got married and went on to have two sons. Mary's two step-brothers, 19 and 17, whom she adored.

Even as Mary had grown up and left home, her father and stepmother remained a source of advice for Mary and many of Mary's friends. Mary was especially grateful for this close relationship with her dad and Elizabeth now.

———— ⁘ ————

CHAPTER 15

Carol knew she could count on Gene and Elizabeth for sound advice. She called Mary's dad and asked if she could come over to talk with him and Elizabeth.

"Yes, Carol, come on over. We're both home today. Mary said you might be calling about Abby and his brother." Gene responded.

Gene and Elizabeth's house was a short walk from Carol's mother's home. Arriving there, it was another beautiful, cool October day, and Elizabeth brought coffee and cookies out to the open front porch.

"Let's sit outside and enjoy this weather while we talk," Elizabeth said to Carol.

"Good idea! The freezing weather will be here soon enough," answered Carol. They made themselves comfortable and Carol filled them in on Abby and his family. She explained how they were living in the U.S. illegally and felt they should be reported, especially in light of April's murder. Had Assad been deported, April would still be alive.

"I agree, it's the right thing to do in this case," said Elizabeth. "I'll call an FBI friend of mine to find out what you should do next. They probably will want to interview you. Would that be okay"?

"That would be fine," replied Carol. She spent a few hours visiting with Gene and Elizabeth and afterward, thanking them for their advice, she went back to her mother's, feeling more confident about her game plan.

Two days later, Carol received a call. "Hi, I'm Agent Starks from the FBI. Elizabeth Campbell called me and said you have some information you would like to share with us. My partner and I are in your neighborhood. Would it be okay to come over now"?

"That would be fine," answered Carol. A little while later, there was a knock at the door and Carol opened it to two well-dressed men standing on her porch.

"Hello, I'm FBI Agent Starks and this is my partner, Agent Williams." Carol invited them in. They sat down in the living room and Carol started to tell them about Abby and his family. The agents saw how nervous she appeared and using trained techniques with interviews, calmed her down with easy banter between them and her. Carol liked their good looks and friendly personalities and soon felt herself relax. She answered all of their questions concerning the three brothers, including questions about their history with Carol, her feelings, opinions and attitudes.

When they left, they thanked her and added, "This is the input and cooperation and observation we need from citizens to help keep us safe. We appreciate your concern and courage it took to notify us."

A few days later, Carol's mother, Ellen, was home alone when she received a follow-up visit from the FBI. "We want to convey to your daughter the importance of her actions. We researched the telephone records of the brother's repair shop, which now has gone out of business, and we found several calls from a known terrorist in Coney Island made to their shop. Please do not divulge this information to anyone except Carol. We want her to know how important this information is to us. We'll keep in touch."

Ellen thanked the agents for stopping by with this information. After they left, Ellen was elated at what she had heard and knew that Carol's decision to turn in the brothers had not been in vain.

Mary and Carol's sister, Barbara, were subsequently interviewed by Agents Starks and Williams, but they could add nothing more to Carol's interview. When Mary's interview was concluded, she told them about the recent encounters she had with Jamal Rahman when she had inspected his warehouse in Long Island City. Starks and Williams knew that Mary was a Lieutenant in the City Fire Department and they were more than willing to listen to her related experiences.

Mary said, "I had an ominous feeling about him, particularly his derogatory attitude. Members of my inspection team were pissed off about the way he talked to me, too." When they were finished listening to her story, Mary asked for their opinions.

"Mary, your feelings are a hunch and if we acted upon it with no solid reason, it could look like racial profiling; like we're picking on them because they're Muslim. Also, your being a female could add to Mr. Rahman's surly attitude. They don't like females in positions of authority. What we could do is notify Immigration authorities to perform a routine inspection of the premises looking for undocumented personnel. It could put a foot in the door for further checking."

"That really makes sense, no accusations would come from that approach." Agreed Mary. At the end of the interview, Mary was left feeling very impressed with the agents.

CHAPTER 16

On her next tour at the Firehouse, Mary was in her office when the housewatchman called over the intercom, "Lou, outside call for you in the men's bunk room." Mary wondered who would be calling her on the payphone during work hours. "Lt. Walsh, Ladder 115, how can I help you"?

"Mary, this is Tom. How are you"? Mary's heart gave a thump.

"Fine," she answered. "What's up"?

"Is there any chance of getting together for dinner some night this week"? Tom asked.

"Sure, when"?

"How about Friday night"?

"Sounds good," replied Mary, with a big smile.

"I'd like to take you to Peter Luger's in Great Neck; you know the famous steakhouse, supposedly the best in New York! How about I pick you up at six? I'll make reservations for 7 o'clock."

She gave Tom her Levittown address and was going to give him directions, when he interrupted, "I grew up in East Meadow, the next town to you. We played a lot of ball against Levittown. I even know your street," he said.

"Okay, then," Mary said. "I've always wanted to try Peter Luger's. I heard about the steaks there."

"Yes, the original Peter Luger's is in Williamsburg, Brooklyn, and has been in business since the late 1800s. The Great Neck restaurant was built much later, but the place is just as bustling with carnivores as the original steakhouse. The wait staff is great, too. There's very little turnover and they can be quite entertaining."

"Sounds great, Tom! I can't wait to go there. So…it's a date. I'll see you Friday"! Mary was excited when she hung up the phone. She was glad that both she and Tom were in the same work group, with the same days off.

Tom arrived at exactly 6 o'clock. Mary invited him in. "Welcome to my humble abode."

"Cute place," replied Tom, as Mary gave him a quick tour. Soon they were in his car, headed for Great Neck. When they arrived at Peter Luger's, the host pleasantly informed Tom his table would be ready in a few minutes.

"That's fine," replied Tom. "We'll be at the bar." Tom engaged in some small talk telling Mary of the famous long wooden bar at the Brooklyn steakhouse. "The craftsmanship was so impressive; Schaffer Brewery had rented the bar from Peter Luger's for their pavilion in the 1964-65 World's Fair held in Queens."

Tom ordered a beer for himself and a white wine for Mary. They had just clinked glasses and taken a sip when they were called to their table.

Their waiter was wearing a big white apron and introduced himself, while handing them the menu. Mary asked him questions on what to order and he was very helpful, telling her that the portions were big and their most popular was the Porterhouse steaks which were delicious because all had been aged on premise.

He said they had more than a quarter-million dollars in steaks hanging in their basement aging at any given time. On his advice, the two of them ordered the Porterhouse steak to share and an iceberg salad with chopped tomato and their famous Peter Luger sauce. After the salad, the steak arrived. It was impressive and as big as the plate! Tom laughingly said, "Not bad for two civil servants."

Dinner was great and conversation flowed easily between them. Mary finally decided to tell Tom the story of April.

"I saw this on TV and also heard it on the radio," Tom replied. "What a tragedy. I'm not crazy about overzealous Muslims and their refusal to assimilate into our culture. Instead, they focus on converting our culture into theirs. It makes me leery of them."

Mary also told him of her interviews with the FBI. She shared the advice they and her stepmother, Elizabeth, had given about the threat of illegals and the deportation process.

"That's good advice, Mary. Look what happened at the World Trade Center seven years ago. It can happen again. I'm not putting everybody in the same pot. I know there are many good, peace-loving people among them, but radical terrorists follow a different code. We are all infidels and unbelievers and it's not a sin to kill us, according to their interpretations of the Koran."

Mary also told Tom of her experience with the owner renting the warehouse she inspected and the FBI agents' commitment to get in touch with the Immigration Department to visit the business.

"Smart! Another good idea," said Tom.

"I don't like to talk too much about this, but it is overwhelming and a little scary at times. I hope you don't mind," said Mary, hoping he wouldn't.

"No, things of this nature and your gut feelings should never be ignored. Don't worry. You're doing the right thing."

Mary was glad for the affirmation and let it go at that. Changing the subject, she asked, "How is your promotion to Captain coming along, Tom? Is it much different than being a Lieutenant"?

"It's not much different until you get a permanent assignment. As Captain of a company, it's tougher with more responsibilities. But so far, I love it and it's something I always wanted."

Clinking glasses together again, Tom toasted, "Enough talk about our jobs. I know a great place for dancing in Bethpage, Summertime's. They have excellent bands and it's not far from your house."

"I know the place. Good to go"! replied Mary.

They danced and talked the night away and left at one o'clock. When they arrived at Mary's door, Tom leaned over and kissed her tenderly on the cheek.

"This is the first time I've been out since my wife died. Time does heal… somewhat. And my promotion has helped pull me out of my doldrums. But nothing has helped as much as tonight. It's been a good time with you. I feel present again! I hope we can see each other soon."

Mary then kissed Tom on the lips. As his arms came around her, the kiss became passionate. The chemistry was there! Mary slowly backed away and said, "That would make me very happy to see you again, Tom Murphy. Call me"?

"Soon," he answered. They touched fingers and said goodnight.

CHAPTER 17

It was the first Monday in November and since the weather was unseasonably warm and sunny, Jamal enjoyed his walk from the subway station to the warehouse. His goals for New Year's Eve were moving along and on schedule. He focused on avoiding detection of his plan. This meant secrecy and attention to detail were of paramount importance to his plan's success.

Shaled, one of the night security men, met him at the door when he arrived. "The expected boat delivery from Ali never came and we have received no word."

Jamal did not expect the crew of the ship to inform him of delays. His men were well aware of his strict rules; only cellphone calls relating to the wholesale business were allowed. All other communications were to be word of mouth.

"Okay, Shaled, I'll have the delivery teams find out what happened to Ali's delivery." The night crew departed and Jamal put on a pot of coffee. He lit a cigarette while reflecting on his operation and the path of life that brought him to his religious and political convictions.

He thought back to the day in June 1967 when he and his friends were playing soccer in a field near his home in the Sinai Desert. They watched as Israeli planes flew overhead into Egypt when Israel launched its surprise air strike which initiated the Six Day War.

The boys were terrified at the sight of the invading force. They were to learn later that the Egyptian army had retreated from the battle because an Egyptian Minister of Defense had heard of the fall of Abu Ageila and, in a panic, ordered all Egyptian units to retreat. This allowed Israel to take the Sinai and push deeper into Egypt.

The crushing defeat of his country and the military superiority of Israel was a bitter pill Jamal would not swallow. The Arab nations blamed Israel for the attack, which Israeli leaders said was provoked by intelligence reports that the Arabs were assembling for an imminent attack on Israel through Egypt. Just a boy, Jamal joined the army to fight the Jews. He was disappointed that Egypt had not fully retaliated.

In 1973 on Yom Kippur, the Arab coalition launched a surprise attack on Israeli positions in the occupied territories, but did not succeed. In 1978, Egypt received the Sinai back in negotiations with Israel and the United Nations.

Still, among the Arabs and particularly the younger Muslim men, the hatred of Israel and its' Western allies was cemented. To most young male Middle Easterners, Westerners were ignorant puppets who killed Arabs to satisfy the Jewish occupying force of Palestine.

After getting out of the Egyptian army in 1970, Jamal went to a cooking school in Cairo. While in the army, Jamal had volunteered to prepare meals for his unit, since he loved creating tasty concoctions and it was becoming obvious to him that there was not going to be any fighting against Israel.

After cooking school, he worked as an apprentice in one of the finest restaurants in the capital. Three years later, he opened his own restaurant with great success. The restaurant thrived for more than 15 years, but still, that gnawing in his gut over the arrogance of Israel never left him.

One of his best customers was a renowned Egyptian scientist by the name of Shabaz. They became good friends, often talking through the night after the restaurant had closed. Many of these discussions were focused on their shared abhorrence for Israel and the United States. Jamal soon learned that Shabaz was involved in terrorist activities, which had been emerging at the time as the only way to successfully defeat the infidels.

Soon Jamal became involved with a group, al Qaeda, through Shabaz's connections. For a year, he made secret trips to other Middle Eastern countries with Shabaz and soon met the leader of the group, Osama bin Laden. As a result, Jamal became indoctrinated in the group's beliefs. He discussed with Shabaz his desire to become a jihadi and Shabaz came up with a plan.

He knew Jamal was married with three children and that they had to be taken care of. Since Shabaz had strong connections to the Egyptian government, he secured a job for Jamal in the Egyptian Embassy in New York City where he would ostensibly work as an assistant chef. It was a no-show job by design and no questions were asked. He would be required to help only with big events that the embassy would have on occasion.

Jamal received a valid passport and a valid non-immigrant visa with a G-5 rating, used for attendants, servants and other personnel at the embassy. Jamal had freedom to organize and operate an al Qaeda cell with a perfect cover. Osama bin Laden gave him free rein as a cell leader. Jamal could devise his own course of action against the infidels.

Jamal decided to leave his family in Egypt. He did not want to expose them to danger or the corrupting influences of the West. He rented a two-bedroom apartment in a walk-up on 79th Street and Lexington Avenue in Manhattan. He was free now to concentrate on his plans of retaliation and soon became the driving force of his cell. He was proud of the privilege given to him and prayed that Allah would show him the way to his martyrdom destiny.

Jamal had just finished his cigarette when Jamal's drivers of his two vans showed up for work. Jamal told them the news that the boat delivery had been delayed. Dawood "Davy" who was partnered with Hamid "Hammy" to cover the Brooklyn-Queens territory made a suggestion. "The weather forecast last night on the TV said there was rain and heavy fog over Brooklyn. Maybe that was the problem."

"Okay, Davy, you and Hammy head over to Al's boat dock after some of your deliveries to see what happened. If he is not there, check his house on McGuiness Boulevard. You can use the phone, but give no information other than it's a social call."

"Okay, Jamal," Davy confirmed, and the two vans left for their daily assignments.

CHAPTER 18

In the afternoon, Jamal received a phone call from Davy. "We broke down on McGuiness Boulevard near the Expressway with transmission trouble. The van is not moving when we accelerate and we are hearing strange noises. I called a garage in Long Island City and their mechanic is on the way with a tow truck."

Jamal knew there was nothing wrong with the van. His men were calling the garage where Abraham worked with his brother, Abby, so their back-up weapons delivery plan could be implemented. "Okay, Davy. I'm sorry the truck broke down. Don't worry about it. I'll wait here until you and Hammy get back."

After making some of their deliveries, Davy and Hammy cut their day short. They reached Ali's Sheepshead Bay Boat Dock around noon and saw Ali on his boat.

"I thought you would never get here. When I didn't show up last night at the warehouse, I assumed you eventually would come here to see what happened. I didn't want to use any phones." He told them of his late arrival at the mouth of the East River and missing the incoming tide. He could not make any time fighting the outgoing tide and aborted the mission.

The Sheepshead Bay docks were deserted. The night boats were unattended in their berths and the day boats were still out fishing. They decided to remove the cargo of weapons from the boat to the van. They removed the five wooden boxes containing two shells each to the van. The pieces of the Katyusha rockets also were unloaded. The rocket barrel looked like it could hold fishing poles and the base plate and range finder were placed into fishing equipment carriers. They then drove to Ali's house in Greenpoint. Davy, Hammy and Ali already were there with the van parked in the garage when Abraham arrived with the tow truck.

Abraham was excited. "I told you how dealers were using the hollow drive shafts to smuggle drugs into the country. I've been eager to try it with our weapons." They all agreed.

Abraham unscrewed the four bolts holding the hollow drive shaft cylinder in place into the van's differential. When the cylinder dropped down, he turned the driveshaft a quarter turn to the left and removed it from the hollow cylinder. They now had the whole empty cylinder to insert 10 shells. They fit perfectly as planned with room to spare. The cylinder was reconnected with the four bolts and they placed the now-loose driveshaft inside the van. They pushed the van out of the garage, into the street and hooked it up to the tow truck. The short trip over the Jackson Avenue Bridge to the Long Island City warehouse took 20 minutes.

Jamal saw them approach with the tow truck and van and opened the warehouse's overhead garage door. Abraham disconnected the van from the tow truck and they pushed the van into the warehouse and closed the garage door. The hollow driveshaft cylinder was quickly disconnected, the 10 shells removed and the driveshaft reinserted. They started up the van and it moved with no problem. Abraham was excited and relieved his idea had worked. Enthusiastic praises to Allah ensued. Jamal, too, was extremely pleased.

"Alhamdulillah! *Praise be to Allah!* Good work, my brothers"!

"All right, I have to get back to the garage," said Abraham, and he left them to unload the van.

They quickly removed the shells and rocket launcher to the designated hiding places that Jamal had carefully diagrammed throughout the warehouse. They were helped by the two daytime warehouse workers. Jamal made a quick mental count; 150 shells on hand, including 30 chemical shells for the rocket launchers. It was almost two months to New

Year's Eve and his goal of 200 shells, two mortars and two Katyusha rocket launchers was well within reach.

The crew had just finished with their work, still feeling the elation of their successful operation, when someone knocked on the door. Jamal looked out the small window of the access door and saw two men in uniform. They knocked again and he opened the door.

"We're from Immigration and are making a routine sweep of the area, looking for undocumented immigrants," said the officials.

Jamal smiled, "No problem, come in and feel free to inspect any of our men." Jamal believed Allah was surely watching over them, because Abraham was the only illegal and he had just left the factory. This gave Jamal a feeling of calm in spite of the official visit because he knew everyone else was legal. The two night workmen were just arriving. The agent asked everyone to produce their residency papers. Everyone did so and the agents looked them over and said, "Fine, everything is in order."

Jamal told the agents that he was the owner of the business and that his papers were in his office. The agents went with him and Jamal produced the documents. The agent saw that he had G-5 Diplomatic Immunity from the Egyptian Embassy in New York City and worked as a cook.

"You work at the Egyptian Embassy"? asked the agent.

"Yes, but I have lots of free time and saw this chance to start a business here. Only in America can this happen! I have all the necessary credentials for the business and an accountant who keeps my books." The agents perused the documents and were impressed.

"I wanted to do everything by the laws of your great country and hire only legal workers," Jamal said, presenting himself as a law-abiding immigrant with undying love for America.

The two agents congratulated Jamal. "If all employers were like you, we would have no problems." They left the warehouse smiling. Jamal was proud of himself for his preparedness with legal documents and his composure for disguising his true feelings of hatred toward the infidels.

CHAPTER 19

After work on Tuesday, while stuck in heavy traffic on the Northern State Parkway, Mary let her thoughts wander to Tom Murphy and what a magical time they had together Friday night. Their dinner at Peter Luger's and the dancing afterward were wonderful. Mary had a feeling that something good was going to happen in her life. She never thought that a man would be the reason for her new sense of happiness, but it was true. A feeling of excitement, anticipation and energy had stayed with her since her date with Tom. She couldn't stop thinking about him.

She would have to calm down, she told herself. "Slow up! Don't scare him away or put any pressure on him"! Still, she couldn't control her excitement. She felt desirable and powerful with Tom in her life, and when he touched her, she would just melt sexually.

She snapped out of it when she was in front of Sheila's house to pick up Toni-Ann and Sheila's daughter, Alex. She was in charge of girls for the next two days until she went to work Friday night. Time to get her head together.

The girls were ready with their overnight bags. Sheila now had two free nights and said she was going on a hot date. Laughingly, Mary said, "Now don't do anything that I wouldn't do"!

Sheila laughed, "We'll see." Mary drove home to make dinner for the girls. She already had made their favorite spaghetti and meatballs and all she had to do when she got home was boil water. She told the girls there also would be ice cream for dessert and a movie for them to watch after dinner.

After dinner and the movie, the girls went to hang out in Toni-Ann's room. With dishes done, Mary went outside to have a cigarette. She took her cell phone to the picnic table and was struck by the beautiful night sky. The array of brilliant stars looked closer than usual because of the dry, cool weather, as if she could reach up and grab a handful of the shiny diamonds. For some reason, the mesmerizing view made her think of Tom. She felt giddy.

The cell phone rang.

"Hello," she answered. There was a pause and then, "Mary, it's me, Abby. I hope I didn't disturb you, but I had to call you."

"What is it, Abby"?

"My brother and I have been detained by the Immigration Department. They came to our garage yesterday, said it was a sweep for undocumented aliens in the area, and they took us to the Immigration Detention Center in downtown Manhattan. We will be held here until a hearing date comes up."

"That can take months," Mary said, trying to sound uninvolved, yet sympathetic to Abby's circumstances. Mary also was thinking of her parents and how they had encouraged Carol to report the Lebanese brothers to the FBI. The feds obviously didn't fool around on this tip.

"I know," said Abby, "I just wanted to tell you. We probably will be deported back to Lebanon after the hearing since our visas have long since expired. Only our other brother, Mohammed, is in this country legally."

Mary used her words carefully. "I know the whole story and I have sympathies about what has happened, but it seems this was a foregone conclusion. It was only a matter of time, Abby."

"I know, Mary, and it is my fault. I was not upfront and I could have changed the outcome, but didn't. I will always regret losing the happiest part of my life."

Mary felt uneasy and said, "I'm sorry, Abby, and I wish you the best of luck."

"Thanks, Mary. I will never forget Carol and your friendship. Please tell Carol goodbye for me."

Mary sat for a while, trying to figure out what her feelings were on this development. She thought about Abby, a good, clean-living man, but this ending was inevitable. His relationship with Carol could not have worked while he hid his identity as an illegal, even if his family had been more tolerant.

Mary called Carol to tell her of the incarceration of Abby and his brother. When Carol picked up, Mary said, "I just received a call from Abby from the Immigration Detention Center in Manhattan. He was picked up at work, along with Abraham, for having expired papers. They will be given a hearing and then probably will be deported in a few months back to Lebanon. Abby asked me to say goodbye to you and how sorry he is about the way things turned out."

"Isn't this appropriate," Carol responded. "The FBI came back again and spoke to my Mother yesterday. They told her they had phone records of calls made to Abby's garage by a known terrorist.

"This finalizes everything," Carol continued, "I have no guilt for alerting the FBI now, and this is closure for my relationship with Abby; it would never have worked between us." Carol paused. "Do you think they'll find out that I was the one who tipped off the FBI"?

"No, don't worry about that. There's no way your call would implicate you, Carol. Their guise was a general sweep of the whole neighborhood that the FBI recommended. I wonder if Elizabeth and my Dad know about the terrorist phone calls to the garage."

Mary hung up after her conversation with Carol and immediately the phone rang. It was Tom.

"Hi, Mary. I sure had a nice time Friday night. I'm still thinking about it."

"Me, too, handsome. How are you doing"?

"Well, I'm doing a lot better after hearing you say that! I just wanted to call because a friend of mine got me two tickets for Sunday's Giants-Cowboys football game in New Jersey. You and I are both off that day and I was hoping you could come with me."

She smiled, "Of course! I have nothing planned and I'd love to go. I haven't been to a Giants football game since my dad took me as a kid."

"My friends hang out at a bar in Elmont and every Sunday they go by bus to the game so there's no hassle driving. They have a great tailgate party. We have to be at the bar at 10 on Sunday morning. Can I pick you up"?

"That would be great, Tom. Sounds like it'll be a fun day."

"It will, and I would like you to meet some of my crazy friends, too."

Mary then related to Tom the phone call she received from Abby and her conversation with Carol.

"Mary, I know there are extenuating circumstances, but this is for the best, for everyone," Tom offered.

"You're right, Tom. I have some mixed feelings, but this is the right outcome."

After some small talk, he said, "I'll pick you up at 9:00 Sunday morning, we can grab some coffee and drive to Elmont. The weather is supposed to be chilly but comfortable."

"Perfect. Then I'll see you Sunday morning"! Mary hung up and went outside for another cigarette. As always, she told herself, "I have to quit these things." But, for now, she was too happy to really care.

CHAPTER 20

Davy finally was at home, relaxing after the very long day. Because of Ali's aborted trip up the East River the night before, they had spent all day delivering merchandise and moving and organizing retail stock and weapons in the warehouse. Though dead tired, Davy was elated, thinking about the day's success and how well Abraham's idea of smuggling the shells in the van's driveshaft had worked. That was until he received a telephone call from Abraham.

"Davy"? Davy knew something was wrong from the tone in Abraham's voice.

"An immigration team came to the repair shop just after I got back from Jamal's. Abby's and my papers were checked and the agents became suspicious. They took us here to the Immigration Center in Manhattan. We know they will discover our forgeries. We are told that if they find out our papers are forged, we could be detained here for months while we wait for a hearing"!

"Calm down, Abraham," said Davy. "They came to Jamal's warehouse, too, right after you left yesterday, but all our papers were in order, so nothing happened to us. If you hadn't left, they would have gotten you there in the warehouse, which would not have pleased Jamal. If there's anything you or Abby need, don't call Jamal. Instead, just call me to let me know and I'll see what I can do."

"Thanks, Davy." When Davy put down the phone, he resisted the urge to call anybody. He would go personally to see them all tomorrow morning.

Early the next morning, Davy drove to the warehouse to see Jamal. "Bad news, Jamal," and he told him about Abraham's phone call from the previous night from the immigration detention center.

Jamal was naturally suspicious about these two "routine" sweeps and his mind was racing about what to do. He would need an alternate plan, in case their plot was discovered, to go into an emergency attack mode. Jamal decided if that was to happen, he would suspend his no-cell phone rule, alert his attack force via cellphone, use a special code, and have them all respond immediately to the warehouse. He would have to give this matter more thought.

CHAPTER 21

On her second night tour on Friday, Mary was called by the 14th Division and ordered to work an overtime shift, 9:00a.m. to 6:00p.m., the next morning at Engine Company 237 in Brooklyn. She was happy. She knew that she could use the extra money for Christmas shopping. She couldn't believe that Christmas was only four weeks away!

During her two night tours on Thursday and Friday, she managed to get a lot of backlogged paperwork done. The fire calls were mostly routine, smoke alarms and minor trash fires. There was only one exception--a fire caused by a man smoking in bed.

On this occasion, the fire was discovered early. The owner of the rooming house smelled the smoke and called the Fire Department. He was waiting when they arrived.

"The fire is on the second floor! I tried to get in, but he has an inside chain lock." The forcible entry team quickly forced the door. Two Firemen picked the victim up off the floor next to the bed and carried him to a clear area at a neighbor's, while another Fireman used a hand extinguisher to subdue most of the fire. The engine team then stretched a line and extinguished all visible fire.

They rolled up the mattress and removed it from the building as mattresses are prone to re-ignite hours after their visible flames are extinguished. Mary saw the victim acting as though he was drunk, a common symptom of carbon monoxide poisoning from smoke inhalation. With oxygen, he regained full consciousness and use of his arms and legs as his central nervous system returned to normal. He was lucky!

On Saturday morning, Mary packed all of her toiletries and a set of clean clothes, including work pants and a shirt, into her traveling bag. After being relieved by Captain Piegere, she retrieved her turnout coat, helmet and boots from the truck. She placed all of this in her car and headed for Engine 237, using her City map of the streets to get to the Brooklyn company. Despite traveling from Queens to Brooklyn and then to the quarters of Engine 237 on Morgan Avenue, it was a relatively short trip.

Mary liked the overtime tours. They enabled her to work in different areas of New York City. Each neighborhood had a different type of operation. Old neighborhoods, new neighborhoods, areas of factories, high-rise office buildings and residential towers were each unique. Uniform filing systems and office floor plans helped reduce these differences significantly and made each firehouse's procedures basically the same. This made Mary's adjustment easier when she traveled to different firehouses around the City.

When she arrived at Engine 237 on a bright Saturday morning, she quickly acclimated to their routines. At 11:30 a.m., they went to a multi-unit drill with neighboring Engine 218 and Ladder 124. The drill sites for the New York City Fire Department usually were large, empty spaces, such as parking fields, factories that would not be used on a weekend. In Mary's case, for this drill, they practiced coordinating operations in a large warehouse for different incidents they might encounter together.

By early afternoon, the drill was over and they stopped to pick up some sausage and pepper heroes (though not as good as Harry's, she later realized). They then headed back to quarters for lunch and to enjoy the weekend routine. For Saturday afternoon, college football topped the agenda, the Firemen especially wanted to watch Notre Dame and Purdue at 2 p.m.

However, at 3 p.m., they received a telephone alarm for a fire at Broadway and Flushing Avenue, Box 718, right around the corner from Woodhull Hospital. Arriving first-due, Engine 218 gave a signal *10-75* over the radio, announcing that they did, indeed, have a working fire, so other responders would know upon arriving on-scene. The engine Officer gave the required size-up of conditions found.

"The fire is in a three-story, wood-frame building, with fire coming out of two windows on the second floor over a store."

"*10-4*, all units acknowledge," advised the dispatcher to arriving units. They all acknowledged.

Mary reported to Battalion 35's Chief, who ordered Mary's company to take a line up to the windows on the second floor, using the ladder already in place by the first-due Ladder 108. The flames from the two front windows already had been knocked down by Engine 218's Stang nozzle, a large water gun mounted on the top platform above the pumps of the engine. This was done upon their arrival, enabling the men of Ladder 108 to go through the now-accessible window to start searching and rescuing anyone in the apartment.

Mary's company, Engine 237, took a line off of Engine 218's pumper. She climbed up the ladder and into the window. The nozzle man followed her, handed Mary the nozzle and then climbed in himself. Both he and his following back-up man, who also climbed through the window, then proceeded to pull enough empty line into the apartment.

Mary noticed as she was standing there that some of the ceiling had fallen down and the surface felt soft below her feet. When enough line was in place, she called to the street on her handie-talkie to start the water through the line. The Engine 218 chauffeur acknowledged the order from Mary.

"*10-4*, Engine 237, water on the way"! They quickly knocked down the remaining fire in the front room and advanced to the next room. Over the handie-talkie, Mary heard the reports from Engine 218 to Battalion 35's Chief that they were making slow headway, due to partially collapsed hallway stairs leading to the second floor.

Mary now knew why her line was directed through the window to the second floor. Normally, she would have been ordered to assist Engine 218 up the stairs. The Chief made a great call. He realized Engine 218 was going to have difficulty and that is why he ordered the second-due to go up the outside ladder to the second floor.

As Mary's company was operating the line in the next bedroom, she could hear the men of Engine 218 operating behind a charred door to the hall. The search and rescue team of Ladder 108 forced open the door and they saw Engine 218 making slow headway up to the second-floor landing.

In unison, the two engine companies' lines operated and soon extinguished all visible fire in the hallway. With the fire darkened down, the units were able to search the rest of the floor and eliminate any pockets of fire throughout the building.

Engine 216, the third-due engine company, had operated into a fire halfway to the rear of the first-floor store, a tuxedo rental business. On their right, they encountered a room with a very intense, hard-to-extinguish fire. They heard glass break and smelled a strong accelerant. It was so intense that the ceiling was burned through into the stairway above, causing the partial collapse.

On further investigation, they noted that the tuxedo rental store must have used highly volatile chemicals in this room to clean some of the returned garments. For this reason, a tuxedo-cleaning operation, was totally illegal in a wood frame building such as this.

Battalion 35's Chief radioed his driver to have the Fire Marshals respond.

"*10-4*," radioed back the driver. The Chief then ordered the second-due Ladder 124 to safeguard any possible evidence.

The building had to be searched for possible victims now that the fire was extinguished. The initial units conducted search while they were fighting the fire. Relieving units began doing a secondary search to eliminate any chance of a victim being missed.

After washing down all fire areas, Mary's company retraced their path to the window to examine some of the fallen ceiling area. Mary shined her light as her company removed the debris. Suddenly, there came a loud gasp from a Fireman. From under the rubble, he pulled out a little girl, "Oh, God, help us"! he exclaimed.

Another man, Fireman Jacobi, quickly placed his turnout coat on the floor and they gently moved the child onto it and started CPR. Mary noticed she was wearing red-striped tube socks which she found especially disturbing.

Mary notified the Chief of the discovery and he replied, "Lou, there's an ambulance on the scene from Woodhull Hospital, they're on their way."

Although the fire crew sensed that the victim was beyond saving, attempts to resuscitate the little girl were extensive, with everyone hoping to defy the odds.

Now at the scene, the Chief saw the body language and expressions of the Firemen. He knew that this was always the toughest thing a Fireman had to face. It was as if they had lost one of their own children. The scene especially tugged at Mary's heart. She thought of Toni-Ann, who had a pair of red-striped tube socks just like the little girl's.

The Fire Department Doctor had now arrived at the scene to check for injuries or trauma to the men. When he heard about the little girl he knew the men would be traumatized. They were relieved from working the rest of their tour and advised by the Doctor to report to the medical office for any needed counseling on Monday.

CHAPTER 22

In a mental fog, Mary drove to Ladder 115, arriving in the early evening. Captain Piegere had waited for her there and now embraced her in a fatherly hug. He had called Engine 237 when he heard about the big fire over the Department radio and learned some of the particulars.

"I'm so sorry, Mary." She had coffee in the kitchen and the men, her Brothers, felt her pain. She would never forget this.

Her drive home was filled with disturbing thoughts as she headed to pick up Toni-Ann at Sheila's. One look at Mary's face told Sheila that something was wrong. She made Mary sit down and quickly fetched her a glass of white wine. Mary lit a cigarette and told Sheila the story.

"Mary, I think I should keep Toni-Ann tonight. Call Tom and ask him to come over. I think you need some time with him. Of all people, you know Tom will understand this awful situation and be there for you."

Mary thought about that and was appreciative of Sheila's proposal. She needed Tom to help her process these unsettling thoughts.

"If you don't mind, that would be good," Mary agreed.

For a moment, Mary reflected on friendships and felt blessed to have Sheila as her confidante during tough times. Her suggestion to share time with Tom was just what she needed and she appreciated the unselfish gesture. She gave Sheila a hug, as her tears poured in sadness.

"Thank you, Sheila. You are such a good friend to me. I don't know what Toni-Ann and I would do without you. You're a true angel," Mary said, finishing her wine and wiping her eyes with a tissue Sheila gave her.

"Don't you think anything of it. I know you would do the same for me. You go on and take care of Mary for a change. Deal"? Sheila encouraged.

"Okay," said Mary, and smiled sadly. Mary told Toni-Ann what the new game plan was and Toni-Ann could see that she was upset.

"What's wrong, Mom"? she asked, concerned.

"Oh, it's nothing, Honey. Just a tough day at work. You'll stay with Sheila tonight, alright? And Mommy will see you tomorrow and we'll get some ice cream together, just you and me. How's that sound"? asked Mary.

"All right, Mommy. I love you," she said, and gave her mom another hug.

When Mary arrived home, she called Tom at his firehouse and left a message. She watched the evening news and a few channels that had covered the fire. Mary's eyes were transfixed on the window they had entered and she thought about her dad and what he had often said. "It's like losing one of your own," just as Captain Piegere had said.

Soon, Tom called and she felt a great comfort in his voice. "How sorry I am, Mary. It must be a nightmare for you. I'm on my way. I've picked up a pizza and a bottle of Chianti. Should I pick up a bottle of soda for Toni-Ann"?

"No," Mary answered, "she's staying the night at Sheila's."

"Okay, I'll be there in fewer than 20 minutes."

Just seeing Tom when he entered her apartment was a comfort. He put the pie down on the kitchen table and put his arms around her and held her, kissing her hair. They said nothing for the longest time. She needed his presence and consolation around her. Finally, he released her and opened the wine. They sat at the kitchen table when suddenly she started crying. "She was so innocent and helpless," Mary sobbed.

"Let it all hang out, Mary. You're a tough cookie. But something so sad gets under the skin of even the toughest Firemen. You need to let it out. Cry as hard as you like." Mary just let go and did as he said.

As she calmed a little, Tom grabbed her hands and said, "Mary, I love you for you and as a Brother Fireman. I'm here for you and, hopefully, will be for a long time to come."

"Thanks, Tom, that helps."

They sat for a while drinking some wine, picking at the pizza and watching some TV. After a few hugs and whispers now and then, she realized she needed to be with this man.

Tom took Mary into his arms, held her and looked into her eyes. "Mary, I want to be a part of your life. I've felt this way since I first met you. But especially now, witnessing your heartache, makes me realize what a true woman you are. I want more than an occasional date or as a work colleague. You're much more to me than that. I want to be there for you, to share the good times and the bad."

"Me, too, Tom. I love you." He picked her up and carried her into the bedroom where they fell entwined onto the bed. The dark emotions Mary had pent up inside were quickly supplanted with sexual desire as she lay back succumbing to his fiery passion. Tom skillfully removed her clothes and his, then smothered her with kisses and held her in his arms.

As their naked bodies melded together, he gently entered her, beginning a pleasurable slow rhythm. Both were lost in total oneness as they began to move together in synch, Mary pushing up to feel all of him inside her and Tom meeting her yearning desire. The pace quickened, making it hard for them to hold back. Mary felt a relief from the pain and sadness as Tom began to thrust harder inside her. Finally, Mary screamed as she exploded in powerful orgasms and Tom climaxed in mutual satisfaction. It felt like an eternity. All of her worries had been obliterated.

After their breathless and shuddering bodies returned to normal, they held each other and stayed that way for a long time without speaking. Mary felt protected and peaceful under the weight of Tom's body. She hadn't felt this way in a long, long time. Later, embracing once more, their naked bodies heating up together, passions exploded once again.

Afterward, as they drifted into peaceful and loving solitude, Mary sleepily asked, "Does a Captain fit into a Lieutenant"?

"Wonderfully, beautiful lady," Tom replied.

"I haven't been this content in a long time and I'm ready for it," Mary said in a breathless voice, almost a whisper.

"Me, too," Tom said, and rolled over to kiss her breasts. They made love for a third time and soon fell asleep in each other's arms.

The alarm at eight woke them both. Mary remembered that Sheila had to leave for work at nine and that Mary would have the girls today. She hurried out of bed and Tom said, "I'll put the coffee on."

Sitting with their coffees, they exchanged loving small talk. "I'm going to stop at my mother's in East Meadow this morning," said Tom. "I want you to know how happy she is that we have met. She loved my wife, but she is thrilled about us. I can't wait to tell her you feel the same as I do."

"That makes me very happy, Tom. You make me very happy"! At the front door, they kissed and hurried to their cars.

CHAPTER 23

On the first Monday in December, Jamal arrived, as usual, very early at the warehouse. The two night watchmen immediately told him of another successful boat delivery during the night by Ali and his first mate, Sammy.

"Everything went smoothly," one of them said.

"Good job! Are the delivery vans filled with the retail items and ready to go today?"

"Yes, they're ready to go. There were some big orders that had to be filled, but we were able to put it all together during the night."

"You both can take off now. May Allah reward you for the good," Jamal said, pleased. Happy to be leaving early, the men headed down the street to get something to eat.

There were six men on days who arrived on time and checked in with Jamal about where they were to store the previous night's ammo delivery. Jamal showed them, supervised the placement of shells and carefully noted them on his map of the warehouse.

When needed, this map would quickly pinpoint the locations of ordinance for their operations on the roof. When the men finished placing the ammunition, Jamal gave the two teams invoices for delivery of the retail merchandise to their customers. They left on their rounds to their designated boroughs.

Putting on a pot of coffee, Jamal took out his small record book from his pants pocket so he could add the weapons that were delivered the night before. Looking at the numbers, three or four more trips would complete the goal of 200 needed rounds of Katyusha chemical shells and mortar ammunition. Then, the mortar and Katyusha rocket launchers would be ready for use.

When the coffee was done brewing, he opened the hatch, climbed onto the roof and lit another cigarette to enjoy his first cup of the day. Looking out over the East River at the morning sun shining on the United Nations, he perused the skyline of Manhattan. He could envision the rockets screaming across the sky toward Times Square. The immensity of the plan was beyond his wildest aspirations. He had faith and Allah's blessings that he would pull it off.

The news of Abraham and Abby being picked up by Immigration was worrying him, though. Were the two investigations--one at the warehouse and one at the repair shop--just coincidences or were the infidels on to something?

Jamal lectured his men constantly about not talking at their mosques or using electronic communications. The 1993 bombing of the World Trade Center proved how careless and stupid the terrorist's actions had been that failed day. Because they used cell phones to communicate, the FBI knew more about their operations than the terrorists did.

One of his day men called up to the roof interrupting his thoughts and told Jamal he was wanted on the phone. He went down and Josef, the head chef at the Egyptian Embassy, was on the line.

"Peace be upon you, Jamal. I have a favor to ask."

"Anything for you, Josef. What is it"?

"We are understaffed in the kitchen because of the exceptional number of dinner parties and diplomatic events that are scheduled for the holidays. Can you come to the embassy tomorrow morning for a staff meeting? I'm asking everyone in the kitchen for an additional day per week and we have to schedule it correctly."

"Of course, Josef, what time"? Jamal respectfully asked.

"Ten o'clock."

"I'll be there."

Jamal hung up the phone; he continued to sit at his desk thinking, "Maybe my plans are being made for me, if I have to spend much time at the Embassy in the coming week." All of a sudden he heard loud talking coming from the warehouse floor. He got up and opened his office door to see his delivery man, Davy, who had returned very early and was in a very excited state.

"What's the matter, Davy"? he asked.

"Jamal, something terrible happened to Ali and Sammy after they left last night. They were in a boating accident! The boat sunk and Sammy is missing. Ali was taken unconscious to Bellevue Hospital in Manhattan"!

"Calm down, Davy, and tell me exactly what happened." He brought Davy into his office and sat him down.

Davy took a deep breath and began, "When Hammy and I left this morning in the van, we were driving to our first delivery when my cell phone went off. It was a call from Fatima, Ali's sister, who told me she just got a call from the New York City Police Harbor Unit that Ali was in Bellevue Hospital. They said his boat was hit by a speedboat. This happened in the East River last night, around one in the morning. He was taken unconscious and with a broken arm to the hospital.

"Fatima was crying hysterically and I told her that I would pick her up in a half-hour and take her to Bellevue. I didn't want to call you, Jamal, because of the rules."

"You were right in not calling the warehouse, Davy. Please go on with the story."

"Yes, as Allah has willed." Davy continued, "When Hammy, Fatima and I arrived at the hospital, we were directed to his room. A Harbor Patrol sergeant was outside his room. He told Fatima that her brother was stable and able to answer questions. He wanted to know what happened and what about his partner, Sammy.

"The sergeant said a passing tugboat was on its way to pick up a sanitation garbage barge and saw the accident and went to their aid. Witnesses said it happened so fast, Ali and Sammy probably didn't know what hit them. The boat sank quickly, there was no sign of Sammy.

"The Coast Guard search and rescue, the Fire Department water rescue and Harbor Unit teams are all searching for Sammy. They also sent out messages to boaters and marinas to be on the lookout for a damaged speedboat and to report it to the Harbor Police. The sergeant told Fatima that he would call her when there was any further news about Sammy or the speedboat.

"We went into Ali's room, but he was sleeping. The doctor came into the room and told us that Ali was heavily sedated and would not be awake for hours. We decided to leave and come back in the evening. I drove Fatima home and came right here to let you know."

"What time are you and Fatima returning to the hospital"? Jamal asked, absorbing this new information.

"We're going to be there around 7 o'clock. We're hoping Ali will be awake by then."

"Okay, I'll meet you in the lobby of the hospital by the information desk. I'll take the Lexington Avenue subway, which is closest to my apartment."

"Okay, I'm sure Ali would be relieved to see you."

That evening when they arrived at Ali's room, they found him sitting up in bed and finishing some food. Before they had a chance to say anything, a policeman entered the room.

"I'm sorry to report that your friend's body has been found further down river from the collision. The tide carried the body almost to the mouth of the river."

Ali began to cry and Jamal went to him.

"We are from Allah and to Whom we will return, my brother" Jamal comforted Ally.

The policeman said that they still had not located the speedboat involved, but they would be informed of any new developments. The officer offered his condolences and left the room. Fatima was upset and Jamal told Davy that he should take her home.

"I'll stay with Ali while he's still awake."

Jamal stayed with Ali until he fell asleep and after he left, Jamal began processing these new events. There was much to decide. Getting a new boat and crew would be difficult this late in the operation. Jamal also would need two more men to replace Ali and Sammy.

Deciding against the development of new logistics, Jamal deduced that operating with the men he had left seemed the most viable and safe. Most importantly, it would reduce further potential for discovery.

The need of financial support for Sammy's family suddenly was something he had not thought of before. Jamal would check with the imam at their mosque and plan for Sammy's body to be shipped back to Lebanon as soon as possible. He would talk to his bookkeeper Shaleed about payment for these services.

Jamal thought about his meeting at 10 o'clock in the morning at the Egyptian Embassy. He would not sleep well tonight.

CHAPTER 24

Jamal was up at early in the morning. With only a few hours left before his meeting at the Egyptian Embassy, Jamal decided to stop first at Bellevue Hospital to see Ali. Ali was wide awake when he got there.

"Peace be upon you, my brother. You are alive and well, Allah be praised," Jamal said.

Jamal then asked Ali if the police had been back for a statement.

"Yes, I explained to them that me and Sammy left early from our dock at Sheepshead Bay to fish. I said we went up the East River in the evening to catch the incoming tide so we could fish near the piers at Long Island City. Then we left at 11 o'clock, entered the river channel to follow the tide, then I remember nothing—until I woke up at the hospital and found out we were hit by a speedboat and that Sammy was missing, and now dead," Ali looked down in despair. "Thank goodness we had already dropped off our cargo at the factory."

"Allah be praised." Said Jamal. "Ali, as I too, grieve for Sammy, we cannot lose sight of the fact that your brother has become a martyr through his death as a soldier of Allah. As Allah has willed, be proud of your brother! We can only pray Allah will bestow us with the highest of blessings."

"Thank you, Jamal, as Allah has willed."

Jamal stayed with Ali until it was time to leave for his meeting at the embassy with Josef, director of events and the head chef. A few feet inside the embassy building, "Peace and mercy and blessings of Allah be upon you," Josef greeted with a warm smile.

Jamal returned the greeting then Josef escorted him to the large meeting room. Inside was a room full of chairs and tables with about 40 members of the kitchen personnel. Strong Arabic coffee and sweet figs were served by the on-duty kitchen staff. Josef stood up to address the group.

"Brothers, I must do more than just allude to the problems that we face during the busiest holiday season here at the embassy. With Christians and devout Muslims alike, we must host numerous parties and our mission has extended to promote our beautiful Egyptian customs and culture. This means we will be even busier this year than last.

"For this reason, I must ask for additional hours weekly from all of our loyal workers. This would require an extra day's work per week for each staff member. I hesitate to do this during the holidays, because I know how important time is for you and your families, but it must be done."

As a group, the staff stood up and agreed to help Josef in his mission to represent Egypt's hospitality.

"Thank you and I will now have my assistant give you a copy of the new six-day work schedule." Josef walked to the exit with a number of his workers to discuss each person's concerns and answer any questions about the new schedule. Then he stood at the door and thanked the departing members for their cooperation.

CHAPTER 25

All day Sunday, Mary's thoughts swung back and forth between Saturday's tragic fire and the evening's loving consolation from Tom. The sex no doubt, was a primal display enhanced by Saturday's devastating experience. It was a powerful release of the anguish she felt inside. The love and responsiveness that Tom showed helped absorb some of that pain. She was glad though that Tom went to the Giant game, she needed some time alone.

On Monday, she decided to call the Medical Office and request the counseling that the Fire Department offered. She felt like she really needed it. The Medical Office told her to report the next day for a three o'clock interview with May Whitten, a social worker and Department therapist. Mary decided not to drive into the City. Instead, she took the Long Island Rail Road into Manhattan and continued to the Medical Office by subway. The building was on Spring Street, right next to the section of the City known as "Little Italy."

The session turned out to be extremely therapeutic for Mary. She told May of a recurrent dream in which Mary's daughter had taken the place of the dead girl. She also confided in May the subsequent confusion she felt about her passionate lovemaking with Tom that Saturday night.

"It was like climbing out of a terrible black hole and then soaring up the highest mountain," she said, looking down at her hands. She explained to May that her elation about her relationship had turned to guilt since she kept having this dream that her daughter was the burned child instead.

"I don't know how to get this image out of my head, May" she burst into tears. May sat quietly until Mary regained her composure.

"Mary, all your feelings are a normal response to the trauma you experienced. The only thing that will help you get through it is time. It's the truth, *time heals all*, but help in the form of counseling will be quite helpful, as well."

Looking at Mary, May felt a heavy heart for Mary and the only thing she could think to do was hold Mary in her arms when Mary began to cry. "Let it all out," May soothed, "Don't hold back. Tears are therapeutic, Mary, they help you go on to the next level of healing."

After a short while, Mary sniffled and dried her face with a tissue, "I don't typically cry, perhaps I should allow myself to more often. Thank you, May."

May told Mary she had spoken to the Department doctor, who ordered a few days of medical leave for her.

"So you will report for work on your regular Saturday night tour. Also, I'll make another appointment for you with me for Thursday. Is that okay"?

"Yes. Thank you, May," Mary replied.

As Mary left the Medical Office, she actually felt like some of the weight had been lifted from her shoulders. Mary was grateful that she had a few days off. She wanted to see Tom, so she called him at work. It was nearly four o'clock and they had planned to meet at his firehouse at six. She told Tom that she would walk to his firehouse, which was located near the touristy South Street Seaport. "The exercise will do me good," she thought and headed out to see him.

She left Little Italy and walked through Chinatown. Mary stopped often to window shop and peruse some of the sidewalk stands which sold everything from knock-off designer handbags, jewelry and hats to incense and tribal bric-a-brac. Mary bought a sterling silver bracelet with a turquoise stone for Toni-Ann. She enjoyed walking through the diverse crowds of people of all nationalities. Her mind was pleasantly distracted by the surroundings.

She continued on Broadway through the downtown business area of Wall Street and City Hall. She sat for a while at City Hall Park. Then, she bought some peanuts from a street vendor and fed them to the pigeons cooing in the chilly, mid-December day.

She walked through South Street Seaport and the Fulton Fish Market, which supplied most of the seafood served in the City's restaurants. The City was so interesting. Mary checked her watch and was amazed to discover how much time had passed. It was almost six and she was only two blocks from Tom's firehouse.

Mary arrived at Ladder 10, Tom's firehouse, which was situated in the shadow of the World Trade Center. She knocked on the huge overhanging red door and it was opened by a handsome young Fireman, "Can I help you"?

"Yes, I'm Lieutenant Walsh, Captain Murphy is expecting me."

He called on the intercom, "Cap, you have a visitor." Soon, Tom came bounding down the stairs to greet Mary with a hug and a kiss.

"We just got back from an electrical manhole fire and it'll take me about a half-hour to get ready. Do you want to wait in the kitchen and have a cup of coffee"?

"No, thanks. I haven't been near Battery Park since I was a kid visiting the Statue of Liberty with my dad. I would like to walk the two blocks there and see it again. I'll be back in a half-hour."

"Okay," said Tom, as he kissed her lightly on the lips and ran back upstairs. He enjoyed her mild embarrassment at their public display of affections.

Mary walked past the plaza where the Staten Island Ferries took the City workers back and forth to their homes. Since this was rush hour, the area was packed with people hurrying to catch the ferry. She threaded her way through the plaza to Battery Park and gazed at the Statue of Liberty standing out in New York Harbor.

She felt so proud to be an American. After a little while, she started walking back to Tom's firehouse. She was waiting outside when Tom walked up and grabbed her from behind, turned her around and kissed her.

She kissed him back and said, "It's such a great City, Tom, isn't it? I love this place"!

"Me, too," Tom replied, with a smile, "especially now that I know you're in it"!

He asked her where she would like to eat. "With all the walking you did today, you must be very hungry," he said.

"There's a restaurant in Little Italy called *The Original Ray's*, where I went many times with my father when he worked in Manhattan. The food is great and the ambiance is strictly New York, with autographed pictures of Frank Sinatra and other celebrities hanging on the restaurant's old brick walls. Would you like to go there"? Mary asked, with a not-so-subtle eagerness in her voice.

"Hmm," he paused, playfully, adding to Mary's suspense. Then after only a few seconds of acting like he was truly considering a different option, he gave up with total abandon. He scooped Mary in his arms, spun her around, looked into her eyes mischievously and said, "Sounds absolutely wonderful! It's a date. Let's go eat, sexy firewoman." He placed her back down, took her arm and gently guided her to his car.

They drove up to Little Italy and found a parking garage on Houston Street. After walking the two blocks on Catherine Street to the restaurant, they picked a table near the front window. They ordered a bottle of Chianti and as they sipped their wine, they were entertained by the diverse and upscale crowds passing by.

The area buildings had all been gentrified and behind the new storefronts were designer boutiques. The area became a shopping hub for tourists, as well as New Yorkers.

Mary and Tom ordered and enjoyed the restaurant's authentic, old-style Italian food. After dinner, as they were finishing their wine, Mary told Tom of her counseling session with May Whitten.

He interrupted her and said, "I know May well, from bereavement counseling after my wife died. I can't tell you how much she helped. She is a very empathetic professional. You got a good one with her, Mary."

After dinner, they walked back to the garage and drove back to Mary's apartment in Levittown. Tom had no intentions of staying the night or sleeping over. He knew intuitively that Mary needed her space from all that she had gone through with the child's death. As he kissed her goodbye, he whispered, "I'm very happy when I'm with you."

"I think this is the beginning of something real nice, Tom. Thank you for the lovely evening." He drove off with a wave.

As she waved back, a good feeling enveloped her and she thought, "How could I be this lucky"! She no longer felt guilty about her initial foray of lovemaking with Tom so soon after the tragic incident with the little girl. Instead, Mary defined their passion as an exciting beginning to the loving relationship between them.

CHAPTER 26

After being placed on medical leave Tuesday and Wednesday, Mary went on a mini vacation leave for ten days. She was informed that she was given this time because she had four tours of vacation leave owed to her by the Department that had to be used before the end of the year. She was thrilled to know that she would have some quality time with her family, particularly Toni-Ann, and her friends during the holidays. She would be off for 10 days, including both Christmas Eve and Christmas Day, giving her plenty of time to recuperate after experiencing the traumatic event of her last fire.

Her first call was to Sheila to tell her the good news.

"Since you have weekends off, I would like it if we could take the girls into Manhattan over the weekend to see the Christmas sights," Mary said, hoping that Sheila would be game for the holiday time together with the girls.

"That sounds great"! exclaimed Sheila. "We could take them to Radio City Music Hall to see the Christmas Spectacular and Rockettes. The girls would love that and so would I. It's been years since I last saw the Rockettes!"

"Yes and we could take them to see the tree at Rockefeller Center and watch the ice skaters, then we can walk over to FAO Schwartz and check out the toys. There's also Fifth Avenue and the holiday window displays at Saks, too. Oh and we can't forget! I've been wanting to take Toni-Ann to see Santa at Macy's. Maybe we could all do that together," said Mary, with obvious excitement. As the women continued talking, it was almost as if they were little girls all over again.

"What about St. Patrick's Cathedral?"

"Yeah, I would like that. Can you believe it? I've never been inside the Cathedral," exclaimed Sheila. "This is going to be too much fun, Mary!"

After hanging up with Sheila, Mary called Radio City Musical Hall for any last-minute matinee tickets for Saturday. Her day was made even better after learning that four seats were available together. She called Sheila back and told her they were in luck.

"Now I'm really psyched"! Sheila replied.

Mary's next call was to Tom, telling him of the vacation time and plans that she had made so far. "What can we do special, Tom? I'm thinking of Tuesday and Wednesday, the days you are off, too."

"Let me think," answered Tom. Contemplating a moment and then offered, "How about a trip to Atlantic City? I have some *comp* time at the Tropicana Resort, so we could stay over on Tuesday night."

"Wow! That sounds like fun! I love the slot machines and maybe there will be some good shows we could catch, too. It'll be so nice to get away, just the two of us"!

"Yes, it will be. The first of many, I hope. I'll make a call to reserve a room for us." As they hung up, Mary thought excitedly, "Just what the doctor ordered"!

Mary's next call was to her dad. She told him of having to take her unused vacation time and how she and Toni-Ann now could stay over with them in Long Beach on Christmas Eve and Christmas Day. She also shared her other plans for the week. "I'm on such a high thinking about next week, Dad".

"This is just what you needed," Mary's dad responded. "Elizabeth and the boys will be happy to hear that you and Toni-Ann will be here with us for Christmas."

After a nice long catch-up conversation with her father, Mary began planning logistics for Christmas week and felt tears welling up in her eyes. "Thank you, God, for giving me this time and for giving me such a wonderful family and friends." She already was starting to feel better.

CHAPTER 27

On Monday, Jamal arrived at the warehouse at eight in the morning to relieve his two night watchmen. They told him that all of the day's deliveries had been removed from their stock and were ready for loading into the vans. Jamal checked the invoices against the stacked items and saw that they were correct. They would be loaded into the vans by the day crew when they arrived.

After the two night watchmen left, Jamal made a pot of coffee. While savoring the strong brew, he reflected on his progress with the operation. His work Saturday at the embassy went well. He enjoyed being in their kitchen and was happy to know that only two Saturdays were left until New Year's Eve. Next Saturday would be Christmas Eve and that left only the final Friday on New Year's Eve day before activation of the attack. He would request to work an alternate day at the embassy, leaving him available at the warehouse for their New Year's operation.

The two van teams arrived and he was surprised to see Ali wearing a soft cast on his arm accompanying them. Ali had spent two days in the hospital recovering from his boating accident. After the vans were loaded and the teams left, Jamal prepared a cup of coffee for both himself and Ali.

As they sat down, Ali smiled and said, "I'm so glad to be here. I hope I can still be a part of the team."

Jamal thought for a moment and then replied, "When I went through our overall procedures, I saw that all of our operations are covered except one key position, which I overlooked. We need a forward observer. The very important aspect of success or failure weighs on having someone placed in Times Square to monitor and adjust the accuracy of our mortar and Katyusha shells if necessary.

At that point of the operation, the precaution against cell phone usage no longer exists and you could use your cell to relay any adjustments in the shelling that is needed. Do you think you could handle this vital role"? Jamal asked, knowing that Ali could do it.

"As Allah has willed! I can be a part of our holy mission! Of course, I can handle that. What do I have to do"? Ali was elated.

"Here's the plan, Ali. I want you to drive over the 59th Street Bridge and when you get to the Queens shore line of the river, activate your odometer in the car and check the mileage from there to 7th Avenue. We have the distance from two of our maps and it's just about three and a half miles, but I want to be sure. We can set our weapons at that approximate starting point." Jamal continued by advising Ali to look for a good vantage point to track the incoming missiles.

"I know a street vendor you could ask about optimal views to observe the New Year's activities in Times Square. He may come up with some suggestions on perfect locations which you will investigate. Any questions"? Jamal concluded.

"No, Jamal, I can do that today"! Jamal also explained how Ali could get in touch with the vendor, then Jamal embraced him, "May Allah protect you."

As Ali left, another man arrived by the name of Navi Zazi, who had a 10 o'clock appointment with Jamal. The cell leader still needed one more man to replace Sammy to operate the two Katyusha rocket launchers. Jamal had checked Zazi out and found that he had more than enough experience with Hezbollah and their rocket forays into Israel. Jamal knew Zazi was loyal to al Qaeda. He was happy to enlist him at this critical time.

"Come. I will familiarize you with our operation and the assignments of the attack force." As they walked, Jamal began explaining the timing, the actions of his men, the locations of all four weapons, the ammo storage and each job that had to be performed. "Commit this to memory and discuss it only with our cell members here in the warehouse."

"I will do my best for you, as Allah has willed"! Navi left Jamal's office and toured the warehouse to familiarize himself with all that Jamal had told him.

At 3:30, Ali returned to the warehouse and informed Jamal of his findings.

"The distance on the odometer from the Queens East River shoreline to 7th Avenue was three-and-one-quarter miles. I spoke to the street vendor and told him you had sent me. I asked him for the best location from a tall building in Times Square. He said the Marriott Marquis Hotel has a rooftop restaurant with a bar on Broadway and 47th Street.

"I went to the hotel and booked dinner reservations for two on New Year's Eve. The best they had was a table with an obstructed view away from Times Square, but I noticed that the bar is accessible to the view. I left him my phone number in case there was a cancellation at one of the window tables. The reservation is for me and my sister, Fatima. She strongly believes in our mission and is honored to be a part of it."

"May Allah reward you for the good, Ali. Now I have another assignment for you. You likely will live in this world, when other men will die from this operation. I have arranged financial help for the surviving family members of the cell. I need someone to handle the responsibilities of returning the bodies of our men when we have completed our Fatwa. It is Allah who has blessed you with this most important responsibility. I know this is not what you wanted, but after the boat accident, plans have changed for you.

"Yes with great regret I agree." Responded Ali.

CHAPTER 28

Mary's spirits were high. She was ecstatic about her unexpected Christmas holiday time, her job as a Lieutenant, and her new relationship with Tom. Now the day to take the girls on a festive outing had arrived. Mary and Sheila decided to catch the 10:09 train to Penn Station to see the Saturday matinee show at Radio City Music Hall, featuring the famous Rockettes in their Christmas Spectacular performance.

Sheila told her that Toni-Ann and Alex had been bouncing off the walls in anticipation of the day's events. Mary also had scheduled a date with Tom the night before, so to make things easier, she had Toni-Ann stay overnight at Sheila's. She could see how excited the girls were when she picked everyone up for the ride to the train station. They were all full of bright smiles and chitter-chatter about what they might experience throughout the day.

The moms, who visibly seemed as excited as their little girls, decided to make it a full day in Manhattan. To make it the best day possible, they wanted to start early, giving them three hours to explore the sites before the show. They took a subway from Penn Station to Times Square. The girls were thrilled by the subway, particularly Toni-Ann, who couldn't believe how fast it went. They walked through Times Square, amazed at the many dazzling sights.

For little girls, this was like being inside a candy shop of diversity and excitement, including side shows on the street with all kinds of entertainers. Some of the mimes looked spectacular, covered in silver paint, standing as still as statues. There was even one portraying the Statue of Liberty. No amount of teasing from the bystanders could get the mimes to move a muscle. Offering beautiful and festive Christmas music, guitar and violin players also entertained melodically, with instrument cases opened in front of them for bystanders to donate.

Mary and the girls ate hot dogs and drank sodas, while Sheila enjoyed her favorite sausage and sauerkraut. The food and sodas came prepared right from the cart of a street vendor. This prompted Mary to laughingly say, "Nothing like 'dirty water' hot dogs in New York"! But she truly enjoyed them.

They sampled other vendors' offerings as well, including tasty treats of knishes and even delicious roasted peanuts with candied coatings.

However, time flew and before they knew it, one o'clock was racing upon them. They quickly hailed a cab and told the cabbie, "Radio City Music Hall." On arrival, they got in the line, which extended around the block.

"Good thing we called ahead for tickets," said Mary. "I remember going with my dad when I was about eight years old," she shared with Sheila, "and from what I've heard, the show is even greater now than it was back then."

They finally got into the theater and, after a stop to the bathroom, they were directed to their seats.

"Not bad. This should be good," Sheila offered, though nobody could hear because of all the noise around them.

The Rockettes were breathtaking, as expected, in their precision dance routines, especially their renowned "Parade of the Wooden Soldiers." They had been performing this part of the show since 1933, when the Radio City Music Hall first put on the Christmas Show. The girls were in awe at the Christmas tableaus, with live camels and sheep, which dramatized the beautiful reciting of the Christmas story.

The show came to an end and afterward, they walked the long block east to Rockefeller Center to watch the ice skaters from above the rink in front of the enormous brightly lit Christmas tree.

"Let's go down to the rink," suggested Sheila. "I know they rent ice skates."

Mary concurred with Sheila. "Also, it will be dark soon and then the lights will shine down on us from the Christmas tree. Come on, girls."

After skating for an hour, Mary said, "I've had enough and we still have more to see. Ready to go"?

They were all happy to be back into their shoes and off of their skates, and they made their way through the crowds crammed into Rockefeller Center to see the tree and the lighted angels down the center of the plaza. The girls crossed Fifth Avenue and entered into St. Patrick's Cathedral.

"We'll take a walk down the side aisle and come around the other side of the Cathedral back to where we started," guided Mary. The Church also was peaceful and beautifully decorated, the alter adorned with many poinsettias.

They left the Cathedral and walked south, down Fifth Avenue, while looking at the Christmas scenes displayed in the Saks Fifth Avenue store windows. They moved slowly with the other onlookers past the elaborate timeless Christmas scenes. The girls were transfixed. When they finished there, they crossed the street to Lord and Taylor to see more imaginative Christmas displays.

"Well, I think we've covered enough in this part of town. Let's get a cab to take us to Macy's at 34th Street. Maybe we'll even get to see Santa Claus! It'll a short walk from there to Penn Station, and we can catch the train home," suggested Mary.

Mary instructed the cab driver to let them off on the northeast corner of 34th Street and 6th Avenue. From there, they walked west past Macy's Department Store, which took up an entire City block. They meandered along, looking in all of the windows at the various displays. Finally reaching 7th Avenue, it was a short, two-block walk to Penn Station.

Looking at the lighted schedule board, Mary said, "We have an hour to wait until the next train. There's Rosa's Pizza, let's go eat and sit down while we're waiting."

"There's the main Rosa's Pizza in Maspeth, Queens, near the Long Island Expressway. I have a friend who moved to Colorado and she loves their pizza so much, she has them Fed Exed to her"! said Sheila.

Later, when they were seated in the train, they all became quiet. It wasn't long before the girls were fast asleep in their seats.

"What a wonderful day this was. I think the girls are going to remember this for a long time."

"Yes," agreed Mary. Soon, both mothers also were nodding off. Mary awoke just enough to show the conductor their tickets and back to sleep she went.

Mary's festive pre-Christmas week continued with her two-day trip to Atlantic City with Tom on Tuesday and Wednesday. The bond and comfort were starting to take hold between them and whenever she saw him, a wave of excitement splashed over her.

It was a three-hour trip to Atlantic City by car. Time together, sharing laughter and hopes for big bucks at the slot machines and roulette wheels, filled some of their hours. Their days also were interspersed with strolls on the boardwalk for fresh air and Atlantic City's famous salt water taffy. The early evenings were reserved for dinner and dancing to a smooth blues band with a sultry singer on stage.

After another sensual night of love-making, they ordered breakfast from room service. During their meal, Mary decided to bring up the meetings she had with Vic Trnka. She described their shared ominous feelings that something was happening at the nearby warehouse. Not sure how Tom felt about her concerns, she asked him, "Would you like to meet Vic, Tom"?

"Sure, I would," he replied. He knew that Mary was not the type to embellish or needlessly worry over something that had no merit. He was falling in love with her and wanted to be supportive of her concerns. He was happy that she had shared her thoughts with him.

CHAPTER 29

New Year's Eve day, Jamal arrived at the warehouse early with his chest pounding and his adrenaline high. The "big day" finally had arrived. He had been focusing on the particulars of his plan since the day after the boat accident, the same day that he called off work to secure more ammunition for the attack. He had 140 rounds, plenty to carry out the operation with success. Now came the time to wrap everything up and give the enemies of his people a deadly New Year's celebration they would never forget.

Jamal went through a mental checklist. The reassignment for one of the Katyusha rocket launchers had worked out beautifully. Two ex-Hezbollah fighters eager and set to stand in for Ali and Sammy.

Jamal had made the arrangements with the two mosques that would help channel money to the surviving families after the attack. The cash for families' livelihoods and for the transportation of fighters who wanted their bodies returned to their homelands had been arranged. Later, Jamal would address his men and assure them of these developments.

After carrying out the day's deliveries, the drivers of the two vans would pick up the 20-man defense team in groups of five, their automatic weapons, and the ammunition stashed at several locations in Brooklyn and Manhattan. The vans then would be used to transport the men and hardware to the warehouse in scattered intervals.

All positions had been covered, including eight weapons operators and two ammunition bearers in charge of preparing the missiles for final deployment.

Close-knit teamwork was of the essence.

At two in the afternoon, the first weapons squad of five men were dropped off at the warehouse. They were given positions and a briefing of the attack plan. In this manner, by six o'clock, all the men would be at the warehouse with their automatic weapons to hold off any unexpected attacks on the warehouse. At sundown, they would all meet for salat and pray to Allah that many infidels would die at their hands! Jamal kept analyzing his plan constantly to ensure that he hadn't missed anything.

After evening prayer, Jamal had a farewell dinner for the men, catered by a Middle Eastern restaurant in Brighton Beach, Brooklyn. A New Year's Eve party also served as perfect subterfuge in case any police were in the area. After a hearty meal, the forward observer, Ali, addressed the men about the mission, with Jamal's approval.

"It is the will of Allah, I will not be by your side but will oversee part of our fatwa that is paramount to the success of our mission. I have two notebooks with your information, your names, addresses and relatives to contact. Jamal has set aside all of the cash from our business venture for whatever is needed for your families. Shaled and I have established trusted contacts within two mosques for help in this matter."

Ali paused, looked up with tears in his eyes and finished by saying, "It will be my sacred responsibility in the name of Allah to do this, my brothers. I am sorry that I cannot be there with you in battle, but rest assured, your loved ones will be provided for as if they were my own flesh and blood."

Before Ali could leave the room, each man embraced him, kissed him on the cheek and told him they were sorry. The men knew how much he wanted to be martyred with them.

By 10:30 that night, their weapons, two rocket launchers and two mortars were taken stealthily to the roof. The weather was cooperating. It was a gray, overcast night. Luckily, there was a light northerly wind and only a slight chance of rain. Jamal and the men all agreed the perfect weather conditions were a sign from Allah--they were on the side of the righteous fighting against the injustices of the American deceivers.

What they didn't notice while placing their weapons on the roof, was the small black bump which was Vic's head peering at them over the parapet of the vacant building next door. Jamal and his men were not alone.

CHAPTER 30

A week before New Year's, Tom met Mary at the firehouse when her day tour ended at six o'clock. All the members of Ladder 115 were happy to see him. He had been a Fireman's boss for many years there and the respect for him showed. The men all guessed that Mary and Tom were an "item" and it pleased them. Tom had a cup of coffee in the kitchen with the men and they traded stories for a little while.

At seven o'clock, Tom and Mary took separate cars and headed over to Vic's warehouse to talk about a plan Vic said he had concerning the Muslims next door. Vic had prepared a delicious spaghetti dinner for their clandestine meeting.

Arriving together, Tom opened the side door to the warehouse, they could smell the aroma of sauce coming from inside. "Smells delicious, Vic," said Tom, as he entered his kitchen.

"How about a nice glass of wine for you folks to relax with, eh"? Vic asked, with a smile and headed off to get it after seating his guests.

Over a bottle of Chianti and spaghetti, sausage and meatballs, Mary told Tom and Vic of the call she had just received on Saturday from Abby, from the Immigration Detention Center in downtown New York.

"Abby told me he had his hearing finally and was going to be deported within a week or two. He was sorry things turned out so badly for him, but was resigned to it.

"Interestingly, Abby asked me if I was working on New Year's Eve and I told him I was off. He told me that he heard rumors of trouble on New Year's Eve in Times Square, nothing concrete, but he was glad I wasn't working that night.

"He went on to tell me that he valued my friendship and regretted how things had turned out for him and Carol, that he'll always love her. He wished me good luck and for Allah to protect me. Bizarre, don't you think?"

"Yes, that was a weird statement. I wonder what Abby meant by rumors," said Tom.

"Well, after I hung up with Abby, I called Agent Starks at the FBI and told him about Abby's remarks. He, too, said he had heard from sources in the Muslim communities that something may be slated for Times Square on New Year's Eve.

"Starks told me the FBI, CIA, along with the New York City Police Department, have been investigating rumors like this all month long due to the paranoid Y2K millennium predictions that the world is going to end."

"Well, maybe we weren't so far off about our suspicions after all, Mary, if the FBI has heard rumors, too," said Vic, inquisitively.

"It looks like something could be up, but what," replied Tom, "and what can we do about it"?

"I have proposed a plan," said Vic. "I don't know how you're going to feel about something I have done, but I couldn't overcome my premonition that something very wrong is going on over there"!

"Vic, I have the same ominous feelings," Mary agreed.

Tom didn't remark, but was listening intently. Vic began telling them how he put together four Molotov cocktails and stashed them inside the vacant building next door to the Muslim's warehouse.

"If something does happen over there, I want to be ready"!

Before Mary and Tom could respond, Vic went on to tell them of his experience in the Battle of the Bulge in World War II.

"The German tanks were vastly superior to our Sherman tanks at that time. Their heavy armor and superior fire power gave our tank corps a hard time. So, we decided to make Molotov cocktails from discarded bottles we found in local towns.

"The German tanks were forced to slow up when they encountered heavy foliage in the forests or dense hedgerows that separated properties. As they slowed up, we threw the cocktails in their turrets and at the heavily greased tracking systems under the tanks, which ignited when the cocktails exploded. We were lucky enough to knock out a few tanks.

"I made four cocktails using thin glass bottles, which should break easily on contact with the soft tar roofs. I'm working here New Year's Eve for another stationary engineer. I've secured night binoculars from a friend of mine in the army reserves, I can use them to spot any activity. You're welcome to join me if you feel the way I do about this situation."

Mary and Tom were silent. Mary knew how she felt and was wondering about Tom. "How do you feel, Tom"?

Tom was reflective and then he spoke.

"I know how you both feel and though I do not have the same strong hunches, I don't want the both of you doing this without me. If nothing happens, nothing is lost. But if something were to happen, I'd want to be with you."

"I've devised a plan of action. Tell me what you think of it," said Vic and took out a diagram he made.

"About 10 o'clock New Year's Eve, we'll enter the vacant building next to their warehouse. I'll have black ski cap and black clothing on. I'll crawl on the roof to the end nearest the East River, here," Vic said pointing to the area on his diagram, "If I spot attack activity with my binoculars, I will crawl back to you at the scuttle ladder to the roof.

"The cocktails will be hidden in the factory near the ladder leading to the roof. Tom, you'll take two of the cocktails and move onto the roof to the front of the building. Ignite the first cocktail and throw it over their canopy so it lands on the far side of their roof. This will confuse them about where it came from.

"Then, move toward the river until you are even with the canopy, ignite and throw the second cocktail so it lands in front of the canopy. Then crawl back to Mary at the scuttle ladder. She'll have the other two cocktails.

"Both of you ignite one and throw it in unison to the area just in front of the first two cocktails. Finally, get the hell out of there, staying low under the parapet and out of sight. The three of us will be out the door and headed toward my building."

Vic sat back. "Have I missed anything? What do you think"?

They sat there quiet and pondered the plan of attack. Tom spoke first.

"Vic, I think you're in over your head, but it's crazy enough to work if there is terrorist activity on their rooftop New Year's Eve. How about you, Mary"?

"It sounds dangerous, but feasible. Count me in."

They talked for a while and discussed additional logistics. After about an hour later, Vic asked if they could come by at 9:30 on New Year's Eve.

"We'll be here," Mary and Tom answered in unison.

The three said good night and left. Once outside, Mary and Tom decided to drive their cars to a diner near Mary's home. They sat at a table with coffee and at first said nothing. Tom spoke first.

"Mary, I think it's a sound plan and I look at it this way. If we decided to do nothing and something tragic happened, we'd never forgive ourselves."

"I agree," said Mary.

They walked to their cars in the lot and embraced, saying nothing. Finally, Mary looked deep into Tom's eyes, "I'm so relieved that you're with me and on this."

Tom held her tightly to his chest and whispered in her ear, "I know, Mary. I know. I'm here for you."

CHAPTER 31

Mary and Tom worked from nine to six p.m. on New Year's Eve day. Tom's was an overtime tour and Mary's tour was a mutual exchange with another young Lieutenant, who had a planned New Year's Eve weekend away. They decided to meet at Harry Galleo's Italian Deli-Restaurant at seven o'clock in Long Island City, have dinner and then go on to meet Vic at his frozen food warehouse which was just three blocks away.

Harry enthusiastically greeted them at the door when they arrived, he was happy to see them.

"I hope you're here to eat"! he exclaimed, in a slight Italian accent. The place was full, "I always keep a table in case special people show up. I have one just for you, right near the window, looking out at the bocce court. It's fun to watch the guys play."

"Thanks, Harry, what do you recommend we eat"? asked Tom.

"Our rib roast beef was cooked fresh today. It's delicious"!

Tom replied, "Sounds good. I'd like an end piece."

"Excellent! You also may want to try my special for tonight, fresh-made calamari and scungilli salad or the pasta fagioli. How about some homemade red wine and fresh baked bread to start"?

They laughed. "Bring it all on, Harry. We're hungry and it's our last meal of the year"!

While sipping their wine, they observed the old ethnic Italian crowd around them. Whenever anyone looked over at their table, their glasses would raise in a mutual toast for the New Year. The atmosphere was festive. Looking through the window, they noticed the usual, animated crowds, watching the bocce match.

"You'd be surprised at how much money is bet on these games. No penny ante bets here," said Tom.

"What an atmosphere here," answered Mary. "I'll bet they'll never see the Times Square ball drop. They'll probably be worn out and in bed before that"!

"Yeah, this neighborhood is old-school," replied Tom. "They work hard all their lives and they party the same way. Don't bet on them going to bed early. You'd lose"!

The waiter brought their dinner out and, as always, it was better than expected. Everyone was always amazed at Harry's culinary skills. Anything he made, all types of food, was always top-shelf. Cooking was a lifelong passion of his. His successful business proved he was a talented culinary artist.

When Tom and Mary finished their dinner, Harry came over and sat down with them. He offered them an aperitif, a cup of espresso with a cordial glass of Sambuca on the side, containing the traditional black coffee beans. Mary felt she was in the presence of an icon, a big, strong, compassionate friend. As a kid, her father had told her many firehouse stories about Harry, so she knew a lot about him, more than he imagined she knew.

"Harry, we have plans to be at the River Club tonight. We've reserved a table to bring in the New Year there," said Tom, making up a story about their New Year's Eve plans.

Excellent choice and what a band and show they put on," said Harry.

Tom asked the approaching waiter for a check and Harry immediately intervened. "Looking at the both of you, I am expecting much happiness and I am so glad. Please, this meal is on me. Accept this for the wonderful feeling I have for the both of you." They knew this was Harry's generous style and they could not refuse.

Mary and Tom thanked him and wished him a happy and healthy New Year. As they arose from the table, Harry, with his huge hands and arms, embraced them both heartily.

CHAPTER 32

When they left Harry's place, Mary and Tom drove their cars to Mary's firehouse, three blocks away. Mary gave the house watchman the keys to her car and explained that she and Tom had just left Harry's restaurant for an early dinner and now they had reservations at the River Club to celebrate the arrival of the New Year.

"We'll see you later. We may even stay at the firehouse tonight, depending on our condition," she added.

Mary hated the subterfuge, but there was no other choice. On arrival at Vic's place, Tom parked his car in the driveway and Vic opened the side door when he had seen them pull up. The three of them went directly to the kitchen.

"I called Harry's earlier and told him I was working and he sent a dinner over for me," said Vic.

"Let me guess what you had," said Mary, laughing, "a roast beef dinner with calamari salad and pasta fagioli."

Startled, Vic replied, "How did you know"?

"We ate there, too, and Harry ordered the same dinners for us."

It was almost 10 o'clock when they checked to see if they had everything they would need, particularly Vic's black ski masks, night binoculars and working lighters for the cocktails.

They left Vic's warehouse 15 minutes later via the side door and headed toward the rear of the building. They quietly walked along the bulkhead to the vacant building next to the Muslim's warehouse. There, they entered and went to the scuttle ladder leading to the roof. Vic went up first and silently removed the access cover to the roof and climbed up, staying low. Tom immediately followed, also staying low.

Vic motioned to them to wait as he quietly crawled to the northwest rear corner of the roof toward the river. He put on his ski mask and slowly lifted his head above the parapet.

"I'll be a son of a bitch," Vic muttered under his breath, struck with amazement. He could easily see without his binoculars down onto the roof and toward the Muslim's canopied area. Vic clearly identified four weapons--two mortars and two rocket launchers--set up with several men slowly moving ammunition from the first floor to the back area behind the weapons. It was far worse than Vic could've imagined.

He silently crawled back to Tom and Mary and whispered what he had observed telling Mary to get two of the cocktails.

"It's time," Tom whispered back. Mary handed him two cocktails and Tom crawled below the parapet to an area near the front of the building and a little past where their canopy was situated. He wasted no time. He set one cocktail down carefully, lit the wick, stood up and threw the cocktail passed the Muslim's canopy to the far side of their roof.

It exploded on contact and he heard startled yells of the terrorists. Tom crawled back below the parapet and stopped in line with the rear of their canopy, lit the second cocktail and again, threw it the short distance. It landed close to the first Molotov cocktail and exploded as it smashed onto the roof. Flames burst out, fueled by the old tar and asbestos covering.

Tom quickly crawled back to the mid-roof area where Mary was crouched down with the remaining two cocktails. She handed one to Tom and, in unison, they lit the wicks and threw the Molotov cocktails over the alleyway, onto the roof. Both landed in front of the other two burning cocktails. These, too, ignited on contact creating a single conflagration of flames reaching up into the night sky.

Amid the alarming yells among the surprised terrorists, Vic, Tom and Mary quickly descended from the roof via the scuttle ladder, down to the first floor, and outside through the side door. Adrenaline pumping, they sprinted alongside the bulkhead toward Vic's building. Just before they reached the driveway, a burst of automatic weapons fired in their direction. The three had been spotted!

Mary shrieked as bullets entered her right leg. Vic and Tom quickly snatched her under her arms and they ran in unison to Vic's side door. The yelling was right behind them. They entered inside and Vic immediately hit the door lock and dropped the crossbar into place on the door.

The barred windows exploded into a veil of sharp fragments, raked with the automatic gunfire. The three of them hit the floor and crawled toward the kitchen area away from the hail of bullets. Bursts of automatic fire penetrated the walls behind them.

Vic prayed his building, with its' old iron window guards and metal-covered doors, was impregnable. The terrorists continued to fire through the windows searching for a point of entry. After a short while, seeing it was futile, the shooting ceased as that quickly retreated back to their building.

CHAPTER 33

When they reached the protected kitchen area within Vic's building, Tom called 911 on his cell phone while Vic checked Mary's wound. The operator answered, "What is your emergency"?

"I'm an off-duty Fire Captain and I want to report a fire on 47th Street and Vernon Boulevard," Tom said.

"Yes, sir", responded the operator, "I'm transferring you to the Fire Department dispatcher."

Tom waited, was quickly connected, and repeated his statement.

"We have received many calls about this location, Captain," answered the dispatcher. "Calls are coming in from around the area and across the river in Manhattan. Do you have any additional information, Sir"?

"Yes! An off-duty Lieutenant from Ladder 115, myself, and a retired Fireman who works two doors away from the fire building, set this fire with Molotov cocktails. I can't go into further details now, but alert all responding police and fire units to expect automatic gunfire from the fire building," he commanded.

The dispatcher said, "We are receiving a *mayday* call from Engine 258, the first unit assigned. Stand by, sir. Listen."

"This is Lieutenant Johnson from Engine 258. *Mayday! Mayday*"! he repeated. "We have been hit with automatic gunfire coming from the roof of the fire building. My chauffeur and a Fireman behind him in the rear seat have been hit."

In spite of his bullet wound, the chauffeur was able to move the engine around the corner at the nearest intersection out of firing range.

"I now have the chauffer in the back seat, too, and I'm taking the Engine to Greenpoint Hospital. Notify them and have them ready. Our two men are seriously wounded!" Lieutenant Johnson shouted.

"*10-4*"! responded the dispatcher.

Following Engine 258, Ladder 115 heard the gunfire and saw the Engine turn into a side street for cover. They heard the message sent by Lieutenant Johnson to the dispatcher. Ladder 115 pulled over and onto the sidewalk, close to the next-door vacant building for cover. Battalion 45's Chief Shea, following in his car, pulled in behind them.

Two police cars from the nearby 108th precinct that arrived with Ladder 115 had witnessed the gunfire and took cover in the empty lot shielded by the vacant building Vic, Tom and Mary had been in. Two cops from the first squad car used Ladder 115 for cover and on an angle from their position, started firing their Glock automatic pistols at the front of the building.

The other two policemen from the second squad car ran to the rear of the vacant building. They entered a side door and inside, observed the ladder leading up to the roof. Climbing up the ladder and onto the roof, they crawled across to the south parapet facing the terrorist building. The cops immediately opened fire shooting indiscriminately at the blazing roof.

Chief Shea notified the fire dispatcher to transmit a full third-alarm assignment, which included a full second alarm.

"*10-4*," replied the dispatcher.

"You have a full first alarm responding now; three engines and two trucks, along with Marine 6 and Rescue 4. Marine 1 is in the vicinity and they are responding to the fire."

Meanwhile, Chief Shea was perplexed to see Tom emerge from Vic Trnka's frozen food storage warehouse.

"What are *you* doing here, Cap"?

Before he could provide details, an ambulance pulled up, and Tom hurriedly directed the paramedics into the building where Vic and Mary were waiting. Chief Shea followed them. While they were treating Mary, Tom tried to fill the Chief in.

"We set the fire to prevent a terrorist attack on New York City."

Tom stopped talking when he saw Mary being moved to the ambulance.

"Chief, I'll have to finish the story later."

He went to Mary and told her that he would be there later. He gave her a kiss and a hug. Mary responded with a slight smile as the doors to the ambulance closed.

Tom went back to the Chief and told him to come with him to the roof to get an overview of the scene going on. As they climbed onto the roof, Chief Shea received a message from his driver.

"Marine 1 is at the scene and ready to operate. Any direction for them"?

CHAPTER 34

Marine 1's quarters was located on the Hudson River. The fireboat was headed toward Gracie Mansion, the mayoral residence, to pick up the mayor and other dignitaries to bring them to the New Year's Eve water display and fireworks at the Statue of Liberty.

Marine 1, the *John D. McKean* fireboat, which was semi-retired, was particularly noted as the *Bismarck* of the fire fleet. It displaced 14,000 gallons per minute from its six deck pipes and was famous for its colorful water displays of red, white and blue, at celebrations in New York Harbor.

While traveling up the East River headed north, both the Captain and Pilot of the John D. McKean saw the building fire in Long Island City, just before the 59th Street Bridge. Captain Rooney radioed the dispatcher that they were at 34th Street, only minutes away, and were available to respond to the fire. The dispatcher responded with a *10-4*, to take it in.

Minutes later, Marine 1 arrived at the scene at back of the fire building. Next to Marine 1, the Captain noticed a police patrol boat pull up to their starboard side which began returning automatic gunfire coming from the rear windows of the burning warehouse. The patrol boat was also in route to the Statue of Liberty with a TV crew aboard for live coverage of the Y2K fireworks display.

Meanwhile, from his vantage point on the vacant building's rooftop, Chief Shea heard the automatic gunfire, saw the fire and the position of the Fireboat and police boat, and called Marine 1 on his handie-talkie.

"Start water ASAP and direct the heaviest stream onto the roof. These guys are heavily armed with weapons and we have to stop them"!

"*10-4*," responded Captain Rooney.

"We were just hit with automatic weapons fire, too! It's broken some of our pilot house windows but the firing has stopped and we're ready to go"!

At this time, Marine 6 arrived to the port side of the McKean, and radioed the 45 Battalion they were available.

"Stand by for further orders," radioed back the Chief Shea

Captain Rooney switched on the water tower deck pipe which was operated electronically from the pilot house. He ordered Pilot Anderson to start water with the heaviest stream possible.

The huge water tower, which could push out 7500 gallons per minute on its own with a force that could knock down a two-feet-thick brick wall, started water.

CHAPTER 35

Jamal heard the yells on the roof and rushed up the stairs in time to witness the huge ball of flames engulfing half of it. He could not believe what he was seeing. Jamal shouted to the men below him to bring up the water hose they normally used to wash the vans. As he stood there stunned, observing the fiery chaos unfolding before him, one of his soldiers climbed the stairs, hose in hand and out of breath. He told Jamal that he had spotted three infidels running from the vacant building next door.

"I fired at them from the roof and hit one of them. We chased after them, but they ran into the building two doors down. It has barred windows and metal-plated doors. We opened fired through the windows anyway since we could not gain access and then quickly returned here."

Jamal listened and with the help of one of his soldiers, tried to extinguish the blaze near the weapons. Pushing back some of the flames, with the help of a crosswind coming south down the East River, the enraged Jamal shouted to his weapons teams.

"Start firing immediately!" He commanded the Katyusha rocket launcher teams, "Use the chemical shells!"

On the back end of the roof, Jamal saw four of his soldiers firing from the rear parapet out across the East River. At the same time, on the vacant building rooftop next door, Jamal also saw two policemen firing at his men, hitting two of them.

Cries from the wounded men quickly got the attention of the other soldiers on the roof, who immediately took cover when they spotted the policemen. The two cops also took cover behind their parapet. Jamal looked back to the rear of his roof wondering why his men were firing into the East River.

As he yelled orders at them, Jamal stopped mid-command, halted by the staggering sight headed toward him.

An enormous tidal wave of water was barreling over the rear parapet. Before he could think, the devastation was immediate. Soldiers on the roof scattered instantly, forcefully splayed across the roof like bowling pins in a fortuitous strike. Some men were washed off the roof entirely.

Frantic, Jamal dropped down through the scuttle to the stairway just dodging the wall of water. He had glimpsed enough, though, of the tsunami-like effect on his attack force. Their canopy had been swept off the roof and the weapons operators and weapons, like toys, were blasted toward the front parapet of the terrorist building.

Down below, Jamal wailed in disbelief at this incredulous turn of events.

"Allah, I beg of you to have mercy on us! Why have we been abandoned"?

Hopes of martyrdom destroyed before him, Jamal retreated to his office.

CHAPTER 36

Deputy Assistant Chief Brown, arrived at the scene and was directed to Vic's roof by Battalion 45's driver where he joined Chief Shea and took over command. When he reached the roof, he saw the devastating effect the fireboat's water had had on the roof. Over his handie-talkie, he ordered the John D. McKean to now direct its hose stream into the terrorists' first-floor warehouse area.

When Marine 1 lowered its deck pipe and aimed it into the back end of the ground floor, the piercing stream blew through two windows and a door, smashing them into the building and collapsing part of the rear wall. The mighty weight of the water discharged by the McKean's brass water cannon, more than three tons per minute, through a five-inch nozzle at 90 pounds per square inch, created an incredibly damaging force.

The powerful stream pulverized the contents on the first floor of the terrorist's warehouse, scattering retail merchandise and the wooden ammunitions boxes hidden amidst them, as well as the soldiers taking cover there, flooding everything toward the front of the building. The terrorists could never have conceived an attack such as this.

Two soldiers scrambled to the front garage door and raised it to escape the carnage. Like drowned rats, they scurried from the building, arms raised in surrender, as they entered into the street. They were not ready to meet Allah under these circumstances. Defeated instead of martyred, with no vestal virgins awaiting them, the men willingly surrendered.

A few of the soldiers would not go easy, however. When they entered into the street, they fired their automatic weapons in rebellion hoping to kill the despised infidels. The police units on the skirmish line made short work of them.

The TV crew on the 48th Street diner roof caught the live action of the terrorist force exiting the building.

CHAPTER 37

Deputy Assistant Brown left Vic's roof and went to the Fire Department Command Post he had set up and contacted the Police Commander via Tac-U, a radio band that connected all units at the scene. He informed the Police Commander, Inspector Slovan, that he had ordered the fireboat to operate into the first floor.

Inspector Slovan responded. "I am now getting reports from the front of the building of results of the boat's operation. The occupants inside the warehouse opened the front overhanging door and surrendered. Several came out firing and were shot down by the police. I can see from my location what has taken place; complete devastation inside the warehouse. We now are worried about the live ordnance in the building and are formulating a mop-up operation. We are awaiting the arrival of two additional ESUs, a bomb squad and also the Assistant Chief in command of Special Ops. Please order the fireboat to shut down as we can take it from here. Unbelievable operation, Chief"! Said Inspector Slovan.

"10-4," responded the Queens Commander then ordered the fireboat to shut down.

After some time, with events in order and under the Police Commander's control, Chief Shea and Tom headed for the Fire Department Command Post set up outside of Vic's building. There, they ran into Vic who had a bottle of Jim Beam and several cups waiting. He poured out three stiff drinks, which they downed immediately.

Vic, an old union delegate, always showed up at tough operations with libation for the troops, particularly in bitter-cold winters. It was once a given, but seldom done today. It was welcomed now. An array of big brass was present and the Officer in Command and Chief of Department walked over to them.

"I have been informed that you two have had something to do with this operation," the Chief of Department directed at Tom and Vic. Can you give me a rundown"?

"Yes," replied Tom and gives a brief recap of the story. "Our thoughts were, if nothing is going on, no one would be hurt, but if something was up and we did nothing, we would never forgive ourselves."

"I can understand the position you took considering the circumstances." Said the Chief. "But as you well know, headquarters downtown is loaded with Monday morning quarterbacks. They'll be asking a lot of questions, you'd better be prepared for the onslaught. Send me a full report of all your actions taken."

Tom replies, "WILCO."

CHAPTER 38

The Police Command Post was set up on 48th Street, just off the corner of Vernon Boulevard, by one of the Emergency Service Units. Police Lieutenant Hank Rich was in charge and it was his responsibility to set up the post and the equipment they carried in their ESU truck. He and his driver set up a big board, a four by four foot display that designated all units and their locations at the scene, much like the Fire Department Command Posts.

From their location, they could easily see the terrorist's warehouse a block away; they had cover from the diner on the corner which was now evacuated. A TV camera crew already had arrived on scene within the designated safe area and asked the Fire Department truck company if they could use one of their ladders to get to the roof of the diner. Ladder 116 agreed, set the ladder to the roof, and assisted the news crew's climb up.

Assistant Chief Morris, the Commander from the Special Operations Unit in Manhattan, asked the dispatcher for directions to the Command Post. His driver followed the directions down 21st Street from the 59th Street Bridge, turned onto 48th Street and spotted the Command Post at the corner of Vernon Boulevard.

He stood in front of the big board and asked Lieutenant Rich's driver to give him a list of the ESUs present. The driver responded that there were only two ESUs and a bomb squad on the scene. Chief Morris ordered Lieutenant Rich to call for two additional ESUs and another bomb squad.

"They're on their way and will report to the Command Post," radioed the dispatcher.

Chief Morris, through the Office of Emergency Management, told them to have two Army ordnance units and a Bomb Disposal Unit, respond to the location to secure any live ammunitions and weapons and store them for evidence.

Shortly thereafter, the two ESUs and the bomb squad arrived at the CP and Chief Morris gathered them all into a circle for instructions. With six units--four ESUs and two bomb squads--he had 30 men with automatic weapons. Not knowing the type of ordnance that was in the building, he wanted no heavier weaponry other than the assault rifles, and they were to be used as little as possible.

Chief Morris assigned five men to the front door, two outside each of the four windows along the side of the building and the other five at the rear entrance. The search teams would start at the front of the building, led by Sergeant Robles, who was the officer in charge, and move to the rear, with the men at the windows joining the force as they passed by. The Sergeant wanted to prevent casualties resulting from friendly fire.

The team advanced, searching the rubble. The fireboat had inflicted much damage to the scene and there were several bodies lying amidst the debris. At the end of the building, the outside rear unit acknowledged their presence.

An automatic weapon was suddenly opening fire from the rear southwest corner of the building. One officer was hit and the men returned fire instantly killing the shooter. An ambulance was dispatched and two officers assisted the wounded comrade out the rear door to the waiting vehicle where he was quickly rushed to the hospital.

The back-up units searched the outside perimeter of the building and found two more terrorists lying in the alley between the warehouse and the vacant building. One was barely alive and the other one was dead. They had been knocked off the roof by the fire boat's water cannon.

The men inside continued their search and uncovered boxes of ammunitions among the rubble as well as more casualties. Everything was soaked in water and blood.

CHAPTER 39

Sergeant Robles notified Chief Morris that before they moved to the roof, the ammunitions and debris blasted into the stairwell by the water cannon had to be cleared.

"Chief, can you also notify the police units on the adjacent building's rooftop that we'll be operational and we'll make contact with them when we get onto the roof?"

"WILCO that" answered Chief Morris.

The stair area was cleared and Sergeant Robles told the Chief that they were ready to go. They ascended to the roof and immediately spotted four terrorists sitting close to the south parapet, facing the vacant building next door. Their weapons were lying in the middle of the roof and their arms were raised in surrender.

Sergeant Robles ordered them to lay face down and handcuffed their hands behind their backs. He ordered four of his men to take them to the Command Post and radioed Chief Morris that four suspects would be brought down. He now took his last man with him and went to the rear parapet to check the two terrorists shot by the unit from the vacant building roof. After confirming that they were DOA, he notified Chief Morris.

Sergeant Robles now went to the front of the roof to assist Sergeant McMahon. "Jesus," exclaimed McMahon, surveying the devastation.

"Looks like the men and ammunitions were blown right to the front parapet area by the fireboat," he commented in disbelief.

Mortars, baseplates and barrels in pieces as well as Katyusha rocket launchers and the batteries that were to give the spark to fire the missiles, were splayed about. Boxes with loose rounds were scattered amidst the debris. In the middle of it all, there were a number of casualties tangled in a massive pile. Some terrorists were still alive, moaning in the aftermath, a few appeared unconscious. Sergeant Robles notified the Chief and began to report what they had found.

"I'll be right up," the Chief responded.

When he arrived, he too, was overwhelmed by the destruction wrought by the fireboat's water cannon.

"We have another bomb squad on the scene in addition to yours and an explosive loading team from the Coast Guard Station on Governors Island if we need them." Morris said to Robles

He then ordered Lieutenant Rich at the Command Post to send up 20 of the Police Department's original containment units to assist the bomb squads and the Coast Guard unit in securing operations. The Chief knew that securing the premises was vital and going to take time with the high volume of live rounds and chemical shells lying all over the rooftop and throughout the warehouse.

The FBI, now on-scene, began gathering information and evidence from the Police Department and the captured terrorists. They, too, took an initial look around shaking their heads at the devastation wrought by the John D. McKean.

CHAPTER 40

Ali and his sister Fatima dressed for the evening's celebration and took a cab to the hotel. Arriving at the Hyatt on 47th Street and Broadway. At this crowded Times Square venue, the elevator took them up to the stylishly decorated glass-enclosed rooftop lounge on the 54th floor. On New Year's Eve, the lounge was closed to the public, reservations only, for the ball drop celebration.

Ali and Fatima were escorted to their reserved table in the crowded room. Fatima had learned of the Y2K operation when she had overheard her brother and Jamal talking about weapons transport when Ali was in the hospital after the boating accident. She begged Ali to be a part of the operation and was happy to now be here with him.

The main event tonight was New York City's famous ball drop at midnight and the enormous festive gathering of more than 1 million revelers expected in Times Square.

Ali was thrilled with their strategic vantage point and nervously excited in anticipation of the attack on Times Square. Fatima could not help but notice the glamorous women clad in their decadent and revealing evening dresses. It was very early, so Ally and Fatima took their time ordering from the prix fixe menu pretending to enjoy the celebration. They awkwardly engaged in holiday banter with other partygoers as they anxiously awaited the attack.

After the extravagant 5-course dinner, the New Year's Eve celebrants danced merrily to the D.J.'s festive music. Ali and Fatima sat at their table waiting patiently forcing smiles at those who made eye contact with them. At one point, they did get up and dance to a slow, romantic song just to avoid looking suspicious.

The moment was finally approaching. The dancing stopped and couples began gathering at the windows to await the ball drop from One Times Square.

They watched the huge droves of partiers in the streets below. Ali felt assured he could easily use his cell phone to call Jamal to adjust the firing distances, if necessary.

Ali and Fatima heard the beginning of the countdown in unison from the Hyatt's guests surrounding them as well as the huge muffled roar from the crowds in the street: Ten! Nine! Eight! -- Ali and Fatima watched the east horizon intensely, then – Three! Two! One!

Amidst the explosive cheers of Happy New Year and the celebration's famous theme song, Auld Lang Syne, Ali held his breath and waited for the first strike and subsequent pandemonium.

Nothing!

Ali and Fatima both waited. Nothing was happening! After 5 long minutes, Ali told Fatima, "I'm going to the men's room to call Jamal to see what's going on."

As he was walking past the bar area, he saw a crowd gathering at a television set. Ali stopped to look and could not believe what he saw. It was a breaking news report of explosions and fire from a factory building in Long Island City on the East River. The picture appeared surreal: Ali saw a large stream of water coming from a fireboat in the East River, hitting the roof of Jamal's factory. Incredulously, he saw all of their attack set-up—the canopy, the weapons and his brothers—being dispersed in all directions on the roof by the Fireboat's powerful stream of water.

"This can't be true! Allah please let me know this is not real."

His gaze fixed to the TV, he saw the warehouse's first-floor overhead door open and his brothers being washed into the street. As they scrambled to standing position, their arms immediately were raised above their heads. A few of the brothers came out the door, firing their guns, but immediately were shot down. He rushed back to his sister.

"Come, we have to leave"!

They hurried down to the lobby and entered into the crowded street. Ali was trying to call Jamal on his cell phone but it went right to voicemail. Since, Times Square was closed off to traffic; they hurried on foot to 49th Street to catch the subway to Queens Plaza. From there, they walked across the Jackson Avenue Bridge a few blocks away and arrived home in Greenpoint.

Ali went straight to the TV. He and Fatima saw the live coverage of the warehouse and the recap of the roof fire, the fireboat hitting the building with its huge stream of water and the chaos that followed. Fatima was speechless.

Ali was totally distraught by what was happening.

He said to Fatima. "Tomorrow we're going to pick up the money from Shalad's apartment. He gave me the keys. We need some to get away from this country. I will take the rest of the money to Shalad's contact at the mosque. It will be for our brothers' families. We have to go back to our homeland quickly before they discover our involvement.

"You are right, Ally. This is not a place for us anymore."

CHAPTER 41

After a quick visit to Mary at the hospital to check on her condition, Tom and Vic stopped at Harry's Place to see if he might want to come back to the warehouse with them. His place was packed with patrons no longer in a party mode. Instead, they were preparing food and hot drinks for the Cops and Firemen. The weather bureau had forecasted a cold front coming in with the New Year.

Harry was busy with his busboys setting up a mobile bar in his restaurant van to take to the site, along with food and other provisions.

"We'll be in the area in about a half-hour. We're going to set up in your kitchen, Vic. Is that okay"?

"No problem, Harry," Vic answered. "I've already called my boss for permission to use the warehouse to warm up the men on the scene. He even said to open up the liquor locker in his office and pass out drinks."

"You both look tired. Here, have a pick-me-up," Harry insisted.

Tom and Vic enjoyed sipping a Jim Bean on the rocks.

"Harry you're the best," Vic responded.

When Tom and Vic returned to the scene, they immediately were hit with the freezing cold coming down from the north. Long Island City residents in the surrounding area were familiar with the frigid temperatures and the howling wind off the East River. Curious onlookers huddled close to the police barricades and yellow crime scene tape to watch the unexpected New Year excitement.

The police department set up portable spot lights inside the building, eerily illuminating the building's structure. Tom and Vic stopped by the warehouse's overhead doors and looked in. The bomb squad, Coast Guard explosive-loading team and the just-arriving Army Reserve Unit were in the building.

They were starting to remove the debris of twisted shelving and stock to the rear of the building where two sanitation units were waiting to load it into their trucks. As they were removing the debris, they kept uncovering boxes of ammunition that were hidden among the stock. So far, all the boxes were intact and brought to the front of the building awaiting the Bomb Disposal Unit heading down from the Kingston facility.

"Take a look at their vans," Tom pointed.

The terrorists' delivery vans had been blown from their parking spots inside the warehouse onto the sidewalk, by the force of the fireboat's stream. They were both lying on their sides.

"Incredible," answered Vic in amazement.

"Let's head back to my kitchen. Harry might have come by now."

Assistant Chief Morris had placed a Lieutenant of the bomb squad in charge of the clean-up operation in the terrorists' building, which entailed not only the removal of all the deadly ammunition, but also the documentation of evidence.

It took hours to carefully sift through the first floor of the warehouse and safely stack the ammunition boxes at the front overhead door for pick up by the Bomb Disposal Unit.

On the roof, the men began processing the carnage the John D. McKean had created. The light-weight canopy, mostly blown off the roof, had parts of its structure dangling over the parapet clanging loudly against the building façade in the strong East River winds. The four weapons were swept forcefully to the front parapet area along with their operators. Ammunition, bodies and weapon parts were intertwined together. When heavy debris was sent airborne by the force of the water, some apparently flew into the terrorists with deadly results. At first glance, the crew saw six bodies.

The scene resembled a battlefield. Shells on top of the pile were cautiously evaluated and removed, followed by the bodies which were later lined up next to the bulkhead stairs. Under the debris, still more intact boxes of shells and many loose rounds were found.

They were placed safely back into their wooden boxes, then transported down the stairs and stacked at the front of the building under the watchful eyes of the police and explosives experts. Even with about 30 men working, it still took several hours to completely safeguard the warehouse. A long, arduous night.

The Bomb Disposal Unit was directed to the front of the building. Three two-and-a-half-ton trucks had pulled up and six Army jeeps with personnel were parked down by Vic's place. The new arrivals--fresh and strong--had little trouble loading the 35 cases of ammunition, shells and weapons into the trucks.

At 7a.m., the Major in charge of the Bomb Disposal Unit reported to the Chief at the Police Command Post that they were ready to leave and handed him documentation of the confiscated ordnance, which would be used as evidence in the future.

The explosive ordnance disposal units, along with the majority of police and fire personnel, were released. Left on-site to safeguard the building and surrounding area was a police security crew of patrolmen, a bomb squad unit, an Engine and a Truck Company with a Fire Chief in charge. This was in case further hidden explosive materials were discovered. The entire three block radius had been cordoned off with crime scene tape and police car barricades to preserve the site. In the morning, there would be souvenir hunters, curiosity seekers and a bombardment of media.

Tom, Vic and Harry spent the rest of the early morning hours watching the TV news and taking care of the men who were invited in for food and drinks. There had been quite a crowd of police and firemen in and out of Vic's warehouse throughout the bitter night. By early morning, most of them had been relieved from duty.

"Let's go have a real toast to Y2K," Tom suggested. "Looks like everything is still working. The world did not stop as some of the doomsayers predicted."

On his way out, one cop stopped and looked at the three of them.

"Which one of you old buzzards suggested the Molotov cocktails"? He queried.

Harry and Tom looked toward Vic, who was a survivor of the Battle of the Bulge.

"Well, hats off to you guys. You are truly our "Greatest Generation.""

CHAPTER 42

When Mary was taken to the hospital New Year's Eve night by ambulance, she was treated for the gunshot wound to her right calf, and was informed that nothing vital had been hit and in a few days, she would be okay. Tom and Vic visited for a while until the nurse medicated Mary for pain and then they left. Mary mumbled as they departed and then she drifted off into a deep sleep.

When she awoke in the morning, the nurse was at her bedside.

"Hi, I'm Ann, I'm your nurse. How are you feeling this morning?"

"I feel stiff and groggy," Mary answered, but then her thoughts quickly turned to her two injured Brother Firemen. Since her arrival at Ladder 115, she had worked in the same groups they had.

Jim Russell had just finished his one-year probationary period and now he was a fifth-grade Fireman and very proud of it. Jim loved his job. Ann told Mary he was in stable condition in the ICU. Jim sustained wounds to his left upper abdominal quadrant that had been sustained when he was hit by automatic weapons fire while he was sitting in the bucket seat behind the chauffeur facing the rear. He had undergone surgery to remove his spleen and had a left chest tube inserted for a collapsed lung.

Ed Beach was Engine 258's chauffeur and senior man in the house with more than 20 years of experience. He had retired once and went to California to become a Fireman there, but it just wasn't the same to him as the Big Apple. After a year, he resigned and applied for his old job back.

He passed the Department medical and the City rehired him. "Beachy" hadn't realized when he left how much he loved the FDNY.

With Ann's assistance, Mary got up from the bed and washed up in her bathroom. She put on a clean hospital gown and robe. "Someone is going to have to bring me some clothes from home." She said to Ann as she returned to the bed.

Ann brought her a breakfast tray of coffee, juice and a muffin with cream cheese and jelly on the side.

"I'm starved!"

Ann and the whole hospital were aware of the news reports coming out about Mary and two other Firemen who had saved the City from a terrorist attack last night.

"I know you haven't seen any of the TV footage yet. Wait 'til you see it." Ann said as she turned on Mary's TV.

Footage was showing pictures taken from the rooftop of the diner a block north of the warehouse. Mary recognized the diner as the place she met Aby months ago. The side angled shots from the diner roof were capturing the devastation that the fireboat was creating. The large spray of water coming from the boat was wreaking havoc on the occupants and weapons on the warehouse roof. Soon after, the fireboat dropped its heavy stream to the first floor. The announcer explained that the second footage was coming from a police patrol boat situated next to the *John D. McKean.*

The police patrol boat and TV crew were on assignment for the fireworks show at the Statue of Liberty for the New Year's Eve celebration. They, like the fireboat, had responded immediately to the scene of the fire. Their camera caught the *John D's* stream hitting the back door opening and two windows of the warehouse and blasting down the wall into the building. The force of the water appeared relentless.

The diner roof camera picked up the overhead front door opening and four terrorists emerging with their hands up and being taken into custody.

Anyone watching the footage would be mesmerized and would not soon forget it. Mary, too, was amazed as she watched the scene unfold and feeling overwhelmed by the culmination of what had started as her gut instincts.

Just then, Mary's father, Gene, and his wife, Elizabeth, walked into her hospital room and both embraced her with warm hugs and kisses, with some relief of the worry they had for her.

"Never saw anything like that." Her father said, glancing toward the TV.

"Your firehouse sure took a beating with two Firemen shot, as well as yourself."

"Do you know how they're doing, Dad? I asked permission to see them and they said I could, probably sometime this morning."

He reassured her, "Jim, the young Fireman in the ICU is improving and your senior man, Ed, is doing pretty well, too."

Elizabeth told Mary she had talked with Agent Stack and he said the FBI will surely be criticized for not uncovering the terrorist plot sooner.

"The public doesn't understand that the FBI is investigating so many tips having to do with potential terrorist plots against us, they're pretty much saturated." Elizabeth added.

Mary interrupted, "They were very good following up with the information we gave them, but nothing concrete turned up. Even the request for a search warrant was denied for insufficient evidence. I'm sure the warehouse boss having diplomatic immunity as an Egyptian Embassy employee had something to do with the lead being dropped."

"Well, Mary, nobody's worried about that now. This is the normal rigmarole the FBI goes though. Monday morning quarter-backing is as American as apple pie. Agent Stack told me to tell you it was a great job. If only people would look and scrutinize what's going on around them more often, our country could be much safer; your girlfriend turning in Abby and his brothers is a perfect example. In fact, the FBI turned up a telephone call from a known terrorist that was made to their auto repair shop. Maybe the call was linked to this event, who knows? We'll find out down the line.

Mary told them that she was advised by the doctor to stay another night for observation.

"I can leave tomorrow morning."

"Great, we'll pick up Toni-Ann from Sheila's tomorrow morning. She's dying to see you. Then, we'll go to your firehouse and pick up your car. We'll have Tom meet us at Harry's for lunch. How does that sound?" Her father asked.

"Great, Dad, thank you." Replied Mary.

CHAPTER 43

After her dad left, Mary inquired about visiting the ICU. She wanted to see her wounded Brothers. Her nurse, Ann, happily volunteered to transport Mary by wheelchair to the ICU.

"I'm sure I can walk." Protested Mary.

"No, it's safer this way. We don't want to aggravate your wound by putting stress on the leg, plus it's hospital policy." Answered the nurse, with a smile.

When they arrived at Jim's bed, his eyes were closed, but he wasn't asleep. He had heard their approach and broke into a smile.

"I've been waiting for you to come visit. They told me you were here for a leg wound. Are you alright"?

"Nothing compared to what you went through. How come you're so tough, Jim"?

She gave his hand a squeeze, stood up and seeing that he was going to be O.K., gave him a kiss on the forehead.

"Never thought I'd be kissed by a Lieutenant." Jim winked.

"They're going to miss you in the kitchen." She said. The youngest always did the dishes. "They'll manage until you get back, though." Mary laughed.

They small-talked a little more until the ICU nurse announced it was time for Mary to leave. Outside in the corridor, Mary asked the ICU nurse how he was really doing.

"He's over the hump, but still has a long way to go. He's young and strong as an ox. His condition has improved greatly since last night. He'll be okay." She said to Mary.

Mary felt relief at the nurse's words and burst into tears. She was glad she was sitting in the wheelchair, after all.

"You've been though a lot. It's time to let that pent-up stress go." Comforted Ann patting Mary's shoulder.

When Mary regained her composure, they took the elevator to Ed Beach's room.

"How's the tough ol' man doing?" Mary asked as she was pushed into his room.

"Been better, but I'll be okay. How's my Probie doing?" he asked.

"I just saw Jim and he's doing pretty well."

"Thank goodness, that's so good to hear. I guess he's no longer on probation. He's now a fifth-grade Fireman."

Ed was the experienced senior man of the House, wise beyond years; he loved all the Probies he broke in. H was like their father, nurturing them and teaching them how to be safe.

"Jim will make a good Fireman." With that, Ed lost his composure and appeared to be teary-eyed.

Patting his hand, Mary said to him. "I'll check in on you tomorrow morning before I'm discharged."

When they were out in the hall waiting for the elevator, Mary asked Ann how Ed was.

"His wounds were not nearly as bad as Jim's. No vital organs hit; he should be fine."

Back in her room, Mary thought about the Brotherhood, a bond that would connect them forever.

"Never broken."

She said to herself, feeling powerful gratitude for being accepted as one of them.

CHAPTER 44

Monday, mid-morning, Mary's dad, Elizabeth and Toni-Ann were in the lobby of Greenpoint Hospital waiting near the elevator for Mary to appear. The doors opened and Mary exited the elevator seated in a wheelchair with her nurse Ann behind her. Toni-Ann ran up to meet her and throwing herself into her mother's outstretched arms, began to cry. This incident, along with the fire that killed the little girl, had left Toni-Ann feeling vulnerable and anxious.

Ann saw the distress Toni-Ann was exhibiting and dashed off to the gift shop nearby. She knew just where those big and bright-colored swirl lollipops were displayed. Grabbing one, she told her friend behind the counter that she would be back later with the money. Returning to Mary, she bent down to Toni-Ann's eye level and with a big smile, said, "This is for you, sweetheart, because you've been such a brave little girl these past few days."

Immediately distracted by the lollipop and the subsequent hugs from her grandfather and Elizabeth, she settled down and managed a smile.

"I'm alright, Mom. I'm so happy you're coming home," Toni-Ann turned to her mother and said.

"Me too, baby. I love you so much, Toni-Ann, and thank you, too, for being so brave for Mommy," answered Mary.

Ann wheeled Mary outside and helped her out of the wheelchair into the front seat of her dad's car. She handed Mary a cane provided by the hospital. "Use this until your next follow-up appointment so you don't put too much pressure on your leg."

"Okay. Thanks for all your help, Ann, you've been so wonderful," Mary said and gave her a warm embrace.

After leaving the hospital, they drove over to Ladder 115 to pick up Mary's car. When they reached the firehouse, the Ladder, Engine and Chief were coming down the block, just returning to quarters from a truck fire near Queens Plaza. Mary's dad waited until all the apparatus were backed into the firehouse and then parked his car near the front of the firehouse.

The Firemen spotted Mary getting out of the car with her cane. Immediately, she was surrounded by her Brother Firemen with smiles and congratulatory handshakes; the looks on their faces said it all, she was one of them. Mary remembered how she worried at the thought of their acceptance of her as their female Lieutenant boss.

The junior men quickly put on pots of coffee, set the table and they all sat down to a firehouse coffee klatch. A fuss was made over Toni-Ann and a mug of hot cocoa was presented to her, along with chocolate chip cookies. She soon snapped out of her doldrums. Somehow, the Firemen sensed her worry about her mother.

Firemen constantly were dealing with all kinds of dangerous and emotionally difficult situations. This imparted to them a reading of people's feelings, seldom experienced by others. They didn't ask Mary too many questions, as they already knew the whole story.

It was Mary's dad who supplied the stories they loved to hear about the tumultuous "good old days" of busy fire companies of the '60s, '70s and '80s in New York City, and the pride it bestowed on them hearing the exploits. Someday, they, too, would have stories to tell and keep the heritage going.

About an hour later, they left the firehouse, Mary's dad driving her car and Elizabeth following with Mary and Toni-Ann to Harry's Place for lunch, where they were to meet Tom. He was scheduled to work that night at his firehouse, Ladder 10, in the shadows of the World Trade Center, across the street from South Street Seaport. He was looking forward to the return of the normal routine of the firehouse.

Over their favorite dishes, they relaxed with Harry. He told them of a party planned in two weeks. He told them he had been receiving many requests from retired and active members for a reunion of the 45th Battalion. The party would be a celebration and absorption of the New Year's Eve events.

"I'm closing the restaurant for the party, so we'll have plenty of room for all"!

"Sounds like a good time. We'll be here," said Mary's dad.

After lunch was finished, Mary grabbed her cane and walked slowly with Tom to his car.

"Have a good night at work," and she kissed him lovingly.

"I'll call you later tonight," said Tom.

Mary was happy to finally arrive home. She had been given plenty of leftovers and extras by Harry, so dinner would be taken care of. There was even enough for Sheila and Alex if they wanted to come over. But all she wanted to do was cuddle up with Toni-Ann and share their favorite ritual, ice cream in bed! It had been a harrowing and surreal New Year and they both yearned for normalcy.

---⚜---

CHAPTER 45

With the emotional and physical trauma of the previous days, Mary called early Tuesday morning and spoke with the school counselor at Toni-Ann's school. The school agreed with Mary that Toni-Ann needed time to be with her mother and talk to a therapist to help her process the drama that had occurred over the past several weeks. It was agreed that Toni-Ann would stay home for the rest of the week and that Alex would bring homework to her. Mary told Toni-Ann about the plans over breakfast.

"Goody"! Cried Toni-Ann at the news. "I hope there won't be too much homework."

Mary's next call was to the Fire Department Medical Office to follow-up on her injury. The only female doctor on staff, Dr. Heller, was on-duty. She came on the line and introduced herself.

"What's my next step now"? Mary asked her.

"Mary, I will be out to see you tomorrow personally, for two reasons: first, to examine your leg and discuss the plan of care, and second, to hear your story firsthand, I'm dying to hear all about it! I'll be at your house around 11; does that time work for you"?

"Yes, Dr. Heller. I'll see you tomorrow, then," Mary replied.

After she hung up, Mary called Tom at Ladder 10 and invited him to dinner. She knew he was working a double shift from last night. She also told him she was keeping Toni-Ann home from school for the rest of the week.

"That's a good idea. I requested vacation leave for the rest of this week, too. I think we all need a break," Tom agreed.

"How about I pick up a pizza, a few beers and some ice cream and I'll see you gals tonight after work," Tom offered.

"Perfect! See you tonight, Tom," chirped Mary. She was smiling from ear to ear as she hung up.

Later that the afternoon, Mary received a phone call from a local radio station in New York City. She wondered how the reporter got her phone number.

"Lieutenant Mary Walsh, we're on the air live. Do you have a few moments for a brief interview? I know you have a leg injury and I don't want to impose on you," the reporter asked.

"Okay, I'll answer a few questions but please keep it short as I am very tired."

He then asks her questions which she kept her answers short as possible. He starts to pump her a little.

"Mary, everybody knows the magnificent job you guys did but where was the FBI? Didn't they know anything?"

Mary bristles "The FBI did a great job helping us in any way they could, they are very involved in checking out all rumored terrorist activity."

"Are you satisfied with that explanation, Lieutenant?"

That remark hit Mary's boiling point. "Look I'm not interested in your media blame game, this interview is over." She disconnected the call.

She decided then and there to screen her calls. That night she told Tom about the incident with the radio station.

"Good job. I've received a few requests at the firehouse, too, but I didn't take any of the calls. You have to be careful, words can be used out of context and be made to mean something different from what you intended." Tom said.

"I'll not do anymore, that's for sure."

The next day Dr. Heller arrived at Mary's house an examined her leg.

"So far so good, I've seen the Greenpoint Hospital report and with luck you'll be ready for work in two weeks."

"That's great Doc."

"Now," Dr. Heller pauses, "Tell me what happened, it's an incredible story."

Over coffee Mary relayed the story. Dr. Heller was so interested in the tale and asked many questions which Mary was happy to answer. A rapport developed between them.

Mary said to her, "It's hard for me to believe, even now, but we are so proud of preventing what might have happened. There is no job like our job!"

"Yes." Answered Dr. Heller, "I've never known any people with the dedication our Department has."

As Dr. Heller got ready to leave Mary asked her when she was to report to the Medical office.

"Can you come in next Friday morning at 10?"

"Well, I can be driven in by Captain Murphy. Also I have a request?"

"Yes, what can I do for you?"

"I would like to have my daughter Toni-Ann in with me to see May Whitten the Therapist, would that be possible?"

"Yes, I'll arrange it with May for next Friday."

"Thank you." They hugged good bye and Dr. Heller left.

The next few days Mary, Tom and Toni-Ann took short trips to the movies, eating dinner out, just enjoying the time spent together. It was a good bonding time for Tom with Toni-Ann. Mary was feeling very happy, she could tell her daughter really was getting to like Tom.

CHAPTER 46

On Friday Tom drove Mary and Toni-Ann to the medical office to see Dr. Heller.

"Your leg looks good, still a little sore?"

"Yes." Answered Mary, "but feeling better every day."

"Come back next Friday for you probably last check-up. Now May Whitten is expecting you with Toni-Ann."

"Thanks, Doc."

Tom continued to wait outside in the waiting room talking with the other firemen waiting to see doctors. Mary and Toni-Ann went into see May Whitten. May jumped out of her chair and with arms extended embraced Mary.

"You look wonderful Mary; it's so good to see you."

"I feel good, feeling better every day."

May Whiten returned to her chair behind her desk as Mary and Toni-Ann took the chairs in front of the desk. May was glad Mary had asked to see her with her daughter. The recent traumatic events, she surmised, had to be hard on her daughter.

"I brought along my daughter, Toni-Ann, to see you because I feel she needs help to process all that has gone on lately with my job."

"I'm so glad you did, we all need a little help in things like this. Toni-Ann would it be alright if I could talk to you alone? Maybe you have some thoughts you would like to share with me."

"Okay." Toni-Ann answered.

Mary left the room saying to Toni-Ann. "I'll be right outside sitting with Tom."

May plied over so gently, questioning Toni-Ann, hoping the child would show her feelings. Suddenly Toni-Ann burst out crying.

"It's all right Toni-Ann, crying is the best thing for you."

A short time later Toni-Ann began to talk.

"At first I never worried about my mother, until the little girl died in the fire and I saw how upset it made her. I was almost over that, but then this happens, my mother getting shot and now I'm afraid. My grandfather and his firemen friends always talk about how they had so much fun being a fireman but now, I'm afraid that something bad will happen to my mother. I have dreams at night that something bad happens."

May kept Toni-Ann talking to get it all out.

"Toni, can I call you just Toni?"

"Yes."

"I have a good friend that is a child therapist who lives out by you, would you go see her?"

"Yes, I would, I think I need it."

Toni-Ann was wise past her age, mused May. They talked some more and Toni-Ann seemed to react well.

"Do you mind talking Toni, about your feelings?"

"No, I like it."

"Okay, we'll stop now; let me call your mother in."

Mary came in and sent Toni-Ann out to keep Tom company while she stayed to talk to May.

"Toni is afraid that something bad is going to happen to you, she has agreed to see another therapist I recommended. This Therapist deals with children and has an office near your home. It would be good for Toni-Ann to work through her scared feelings."

"I agree. Give me the information and I'll make an appointment for Toni."

"Another thing, I have a suggestion for you Mary. When you return to full duty I think you should take a light duty assignment."

"Why?" Asked Mary.

"I think it would be good for you and Toni-Ann if you were on a regular schedule and out of harm's way, for a while anyway. We have openings in Queens headquarters fire prevention, which isn't far from where you live."

"I'll think about it, you could be right. I'm sure Toni would love to have me home every night."

They said their good byes and Mary left her office.

As they were driving back home, Mary thought about what May Whitten had suggested and something else also came to mind. Her relationship with Tom was reaching a serious point. Toni-Ann had told her that Tom asked Toni to find out her mother's ring size. Although he had sworn Toni to secrecy, she couldn't wait to tell her mother.

Mary was thrilled to hear the secret. In serious conversations with Tom, he often mentioned about having a family, she too would like more children. Working a light duty assignment would mean working steady days which would be easier with a family. She had to think maybe her getting hurt caused God to open another door.

CHAPTER 47

Two weeks later, Harry Galleo was preparing for a big Department celebration. He was ecstatic with the thwarted attack on New York City, thanks to his friends, Vic, Mary and Tom.

The event would also serve as commemoration for the actions of the 45th Battalion, the 108th precinct and other agencies, including the FBI. As usual, Harry made all the preparations with the help from Probies and junior men of the 45th Battalion.

The celebration started in the afternoon on Saturday, January 14, so the members who had to work that night could attend. It would last through the evening, so that those coming off work also could go. It was a closed-door event for invited guests and close family members. Gatherings like this were specifically arranged for those considered the "backbone" of the job. No brass or dignitaries were invited. Harry had borrowed extra chairs and tables from St. Patrick's Church on Vernon Boulevard.

Tables and chairs were set up on the bocce court and the side yard of the restaurant with extra ones crowded into the dining room. This was a feast that only Harry could prepare. The junior men from Battalion 45 did the dishes, waited on people and cleaned, just like the firehouse duties. The Probies jumped at the chance to be a part of the celebration and Harry's small staff welcomed the help.

Most of the senior retirees who served in WWII and were in their eighties notified Harry of their plans to attend. All retirees were given name tags with their companies and dates of service. As it turned out, the old WWII vets, their ranks depleted, were the first ones to show up. The dais set-up included their seats, along with Vic, Mary and Tom.

Mary's dad always talked about the training they had received from these senior men. No man's job was too small, the philosophy went. All men were vital to the team. He spoke of the "kink-chaser," the last man on the hose-line when it was stretched into the building to get to the fire area. The kink-chaser would return to the engine to disconnect the needed amount of hose from the bed and help the pump operator, the chauffeur, hook it up to the pump outlets on the side of the engine. When ordered by the line Officer to "start water," the kink-chaser would follow the line to their point of operation at the fire to make sure the water was flowing. He would straighten out any kinks along the way.

The old-timers always gave this example of the kink-chaser to show how important each man's job was for the success of the operation. The analogy was one of dozens of examples used to drive home the essence of teamwork. Subsequently, the new men never forgot the simplicity and detail of earnest commitment needed for the whole team to succeed. The old-timers were great teachers with vast experience and invaluable knowledge.

The 108th precinct, along with the two wounded Firemen--Jim Russell, who still needed a wheelchair, and Ed "Beachy" Beach, who was able to walk on his own--attended. There were many conversations and congratulations going around the restaurant. Everyone wanted to meet the "heroes" and talk about their exploits.

When the crowd finally had settled down, Harry acted as MC. In spite of being in America for more than 60 years, everyone loved his Italian accent. He acknowledged Vic, Tom and Mary's actions in preventing the terrorist attack on what they all now knew was Times Square at the midnight hour, when the streets were packed with revelers and the accompanying media attention.

"That took guts and cojones," he said in his own inimitable style. He praised the cooperation and teamwork of the Fire and Police Departments and all the other agencies involved. Harry thanked the crowd for coming and said, "Enjoy the food. I made it especially for all of you."

The party lasted into the night, as more men arrived after their shifts. It was a time for talking, renewing old friendships and remembering members now gone. There were a few teary eyes. Nothing had changed; from the youngest to the oldest, the job would never change or be forgotten.

CHAPTER 48

"I've decided to drive to my firehouse and sleep there tonight rather than drive early in the morning," Tom told Mary when they left the party.

"Plus, the incoming men will bring all kinds of pastries and donuts Sunday morning. I wouldn't mind waking up to that. It'll be quiet all night, too, since it's a ghost town there on Saturday nights. I really feel fortunate to be assigned to Ladder 10."

"I'm glad for you, Tom, and I also think it's a good idea for you to sleep there tonight. On Monday, I have another appointment at the Medical Office and I plan to take May Whitten's advice and go on light duty for a while. It'll be good for me and for Toni-Ann. I'll be able to sharpen my cooking skills, too, by making dinner most nights."

"Well, I would be happy to be your culinary guinea pig, too," laughed Tom.

He kissed her goodnight. "This was a wonderful time tonight, but I'm having a hard time adjusting to being thought of as a hero. I hope this fades soon."

"Me, too," said Mary. "That's another reason for me to want to go on light duty and get out of the limelight until this all blows over."

Tom kissed her again. "I'll call you tomorrow from the firehouse."

"Okay."

She watched him pull away and again felt content knowing that someone wonderful and important was in her life.

EPILOGUE

In 1963, I worked as a Fireman at Ladder 116 in Astoria, Queens. My best friend, Bob Mallon, worked at an adjoining company, Ladder 115, in Long Island City. Often when we met over the years, we discussed the day the *John D. McKean*, the celebrated FDNY fireboat, pumped East River water onto a factory fire at Vernon Boulevard and 47th Street.

Responding to a reported one-story factory fire at that location, Ladder 115, first-due, had the forcible entry position on the first floor. Two engine companies responded as well and Ladder 116 had the roof assignment. Our job as the second-due ladder company was to ventilate the roof to release smoke, heat and flames, which would allow the companies to extinguish the first-floor fire. Doing so, we cut a 10 by 10 foot hole in the roof with our axes, opened the bulkhead doors and lifted the skylight off its mounted frame, which allowed the smoke and heat to be vented from the first floor. When we completely vented the roof, Ladder 115 and the two engine companies could enter the factory and extinguish the fire.

Communications were not as good 50 years ago as they are today. From the roof, we could hear the engine companies on the first floor, hitting the fire below with their hoses. Our part done, we stood near the front parapet of the building, awaiting further orders. All of a sudden, we looked up and saw a massive arc of water coming over the roof and a loud, tsunami-type wave crashing onto the roof. All the roof debris--the result of our ventilation tactics--was swept toward us at the front of the roof. If not for the roof's front parapet to take cover under, we, too, could have been swept from the roof. Thankfully, however, the water stopped.

Now, the *John McKean*'s pumps took aim into the building's first floor. The water propulsion was so powerful inside the building, it forced the Firemen out the front entrance, scattering them into the street as the intense heat and smoke were pushed out the front door with them.

From Bob's recollection on the ground that day, he related how the East River water that spewed from the fireboat's deck pipe onto Vernon Boulevard had the noxious smell of the dirty river water, while small, broken-up, empty clam shells littered the street. (Before the 1972 Clean Water Act, the East River was notoriously polluted, fish could not thrive and the unregulated dumping and waste that poured into the river was filthy and toxic.)

Eventually, the *McKean*'s pumps were shut down and the companies on the ground extinguished the remaining fire. This remarkable event back in 1963 was the inspirational seed for the story you have just read.

AUTHOR'S NOTE

The *John D. McKean*

The *John D. McKean* fireboat was commissioned in 1954. Fifty years later, it was retired in 2004.

The fireboat's water power with its six deck pipes could put out 9500 gallons per minute or 80,000 pounds of water per minute, through a five-inch nozzle at 90 pounds per square inch. The water pump was so powerful, it could knock down a two-foot-thick brick wall.

The boat's most historic fire was an oil tanker collision underneath the Verrazano Bridge in 1973. A ship T-boned the oil tanker as the tide moved both of them closer together, which created a 45-degree angle opening between the two vessels. Upon collision, the tanker released 31,000 barrels of crude oil into the river, engulfing the area in flames and scorching the underbelly of the bridge.

The *John D. McKean* pilot was able to navigate into the middle of this dangerous angle and put its six deck pipes to work: three powerful arcs of water to each ship. Remarkably, the fireboat eventually cooled down the flames below their ignition point and the fires were extinguished.

This unprecedented incident was the first known vessel salvage of this kind in the history of ships and fuel tankers. As a result of the *John D. McKean*'s tour de force, a system of extinguishment was created.

AUTHOR'S NOTE

My book does not condemn Islamic beliefs. Instead, it dishonors radical Muslim terroristic acts. Not long ago and still today, a group of infamous American terrorists, the Ku Klux Klan, oppressed ethnic groups they wantonly despised by murdering, pillaging and raping innocent civilians. The KKK helped substantiate its acts of terror by hiding behind their religion, Christianity. In the same way, Muslim terrorists today distort Islam to support their hatred and intolerance to fellow human beings whose spiritual experience and religious doctrines differ from their own.

Made in the USA
Columbia, SC
25 April 2022

59451213R00117